Chapter One

The five men all wore hoods to cover their faces; they rode horses rented from the local livery barn. Holes in the black hoods let the men see. Since there were no holes for their mouths, the hoods distorted and changed the sound of the men's voices so they could hardly recognize each other.

"Let's get it done," the largest of the men barked.

They had swept down on the small house at the edge of the high country town called Gold Ledge and grabbed Lester Davis when he came out of the house at dusk to tend to his small flock of chickens.

One of them roped the young man and dragged him 20 feet across the rocky ground. Then they tied the victim's hands together behind him and threw him over the spare horse they had brought.

Dirk Fletcher

The man screeched out a yell of fury before they could gag him. A woman heard the scream and darted out the kitchen door. The hooded men ignored her and rode off easy to show their contempt.

A few minutes later, they sat at a big oak tree a mile from town along the ridge trail that led on west to Colorado Springs. The smallest man held a 40-foot-long rope.

"Let's get on with it," the big man said again.

The hooded men dismounted. One threw the rope over a sturdy oak branch ten feet off the ground. The hangman's knot with 13 coils had been tied the night before when the five decided that the task of cleansing the town had to be done.

"I lost me a brother and my dad to them damned Southern rebels," one of the men had said the previous night. "We don't want nothing to do with them bastards around Gold Ledge."

Another man had spoken up at the meeting, where the lamp was kept low and the voices soft and filled with emotion. "My uncle went down at Gettysburg. Never ain't gonna forget that. Some reb bayoneted him twenty times."

They had made the rounds, giving each man a turn to talk and support or oppose the motion. Later the matter was voted on and passed unanimously.

Now in the Colorado darkness of August, one man took the gag out of the rebel's mouth and set him backward on the horse without a saddle. Davis's hands were still tied behind him but his feet were free.

One of the men held the horse by the bridle so it wouldn't skitter away before they were ready.

Gold Ledge Gold Diggers

Another hooded man rode up and slipped the noose over the rebel's head. The young man got the last of the dryness out of his mouth from the gag so he could talk.

"What'd I do to y'all?" Davis asked. "I don't understand. Please tell me how I hurt any of y'all."

The hooded men stared at him in the darkness. Only a sliver of a moon showed in the eastern sky.

"You and your kind hurt us all," the largest man said. "We don't want your kind around here. We don't like Southern trash in our town. The fire in your house didn't discourage you none. So if we hang one of you, we figure the rest of you'll clear out. We don't want Southern filth like you in Gold Ledge."

"But I didn't do anything to you," the young man screamed. "Why me? I got me a wife. I warn't even in the war. You're hanging an innocent man. Don't that mean anything to any of you? Ain't there one of you who's man enough to stand up and stop this. You're murdering an innocent man. Can't you see that?"

One of the robed men swung the butt of his six-gun so it thudded into the bound man's side. The prisoner brayed in fury and pain.

"Shut up, boy. Just shut up and die like a man."

"None of you are men," the Southerner bellowed. Tears streamed down his face since he realized he was close to dying. "You're sadistic ignorant animals. I should never had stopped here. You're all trash, riffraff, the dregs of society. I hope y'all die for what you're doing here. So help me God, I hope you all pay the price for murder and I hope it's a slow painful death for each one of you."

The hooded man at the trunk of the oak tied the rope off as tightly as he could pull it. Even with the stretch it should keep the man's feet off the ground.

"Shut up, boy. I told you once before," the big man said.

"Why? You might cheat me or beat me up? We're past that, aren't we? You're the vigilante committee I heard about. I didn't think intelligent, rational men could—"

The big man behind the horse slapped the animal's rump with both his hands and the sorrel surged forward. Lester Davis slid off the horse's rump and dropped two feet before the rope held and there was a sharp crack all the hooded men could hear as the big knot on the noose snapped the rebel's head suddenly sideways and broke his neck. His feet twitched, one knee jerked, and then the leg came down beside the other one. His eyes flew wide open and stayed that way as his tongue came out of his mouth and his whole body continued to twitch in death spasms for half a minute.

None of the five hooded men moved. They all waited for someone else to declare it over. No one did. After a while, they found their horses, climbed into the saddles, and rode back toward Gold Ledge's lights in the distance. One of them led the extra horse.

Nobody said a word on the mile ride to town. They split up, each taking off his hood and pushing it inside his jacket so no one could see it. The men arrived singly at the back gate of the livery stable's pasture and turned his horse inside, saddle and all, as had been arranged by letter.

Meanwhile, at the small frame house on the edge of town, the chickens gave up waiting for their grain and settled down for the night. Inside the starkly furnished living room, a tearstained young woman worked over a letter. Two other women sat with her. All had been crying.

They conferred on the wording of the message, and when it was done, they all signed it, then put it in an envelope and wrote the address on the outside:

Senator Marcus J. Benoit
The U.S. Senate Building
Washington, D C

"Won't do no good, Charlotte," the heavy woman said. "Nobody pays no attention to letters like this no more. Knew we should have stayed in Alabama. At least we had kin there."

"This letter has to be read and then somebody's just got to come and help us," Charlotte Davis, the small woman who had written the letter, said. "I don't aim to let them vigilantes murder my Lester and go free. There has to be some justice in this land."

The third woman still couldn't talk. She simply sat there and shook her head, then buried her face in the new widow's shoulder and cried again.

Charlotte Davis stared at the letter in her hands. She'd mail it first thing in the morning. She looked out through red eyes and blinked back new tears.

"I screamed and screamed and they didn't even look at me. Just rode right past me. I run into the house to get the six-gun but I didn't know if it was loaded or not. When I got outside they were riding away. I followed them. They walked their horses. I kept quiet and walked behind them to that tree—the big oak out on the west road. I never want to see that tree again."

"Whit and Jeremy left a while ago to go bring Lester back here," the large woman said. "We won't let them have the satisfaction of seeing him hanging there in the daylight."

"We bury him tonight," Charlotte said. "Then they can't desecrate his grave. We'll do it. I'll get the shovel and start digging. I want my Lester buried before the sun comes up."

Charlotte Davis was through crying. She caught up the shovel and walked to the back edge of their small place in town and began to dig. Why had Lester and she ever come here? They had thought things were bad in Alabama after the war. But it hadn't been nearly as bad as the Northerners had made it for them here. What was she going to do?

She had no husband. She could stay with the Towerses for a time. They had no children yet. Oh, God, but it had hurt watching those men hang Lester. Dear Lord, what in heaven's name was she going to do?

The telegram caught up with Spur McCoy when he checked in at his favorite hotel in Denver. As usual, the general had sent telegrams to him at four locations, hoping that he'd be at one of them. Spur had just finished an untidy job of tracking down a bank robber; the case had ended in the death of the bandit by his own hand. Spur always hated that kind of a solution, though it was effective, practical, and inexpensive for the U.S. Government.

Spur McCoy was a Secret Service agent assigned to the western half of the U.S. He usually had his hands full. The clerk at the Meridian Hotel grinned when he handed Spur the envelope. The agent had been at the hotel often in the last few years, so many of the employees knew him.

"Good to have you back with us again, Mr. McCoy," the clerk said. "I hope this telegram doesn't mean you'll be leaving us. It came this morning with instructions to hold it a week pending your arrival."

Spur thanked the clerk, took his room key, his rifle, and carpetbag, and went up to his room. He hadn't even asked for his favorite room, but he got 212 anyway. He dropped his bag on the floor, stood the Winchester against the wall next to the door and fell facedown on the bed.

He needed a good 24 hours to catch up on his sleep and unwind, but he knew there wasn't a chance in Washington that it would happen. Gen. Halleck had another assignment for him, that was certain. He'd have just a small nap before he opened the wire.

Spur lay there for five minutes. He'd only had two hours of sleep the night before but he knew he couldn't go to sleep now. He opened one green eye and looked at the yellow envelope of the telegram. Couldn't be important. He closed the eye.

A moment later both eyes zapped open and Spur sighed, reached for the wire, and sat up as he tore open the envelope.

TO SPUR McCOY, MERIDIAN HOTEL, DENVER, COLORADO. TAKE UP THIS

NEW ASSIGNMENT SOON AS POSSIBLE. PATTERN OF CIVIL UNREST, VIGILANTISM, SOUTHERNER HARASSMENT IN SMALL MINING TOWN OF GOLD LEDGE NEAR COLORADO SPRINGS. PROCEED THERE AT ONCE. CONTACT MRS. CHARLOTTE DAVIS, WIDOW. HUSBAND LYNCHED BY VIGILANTES JUNE 3. HIGH-LEVEL SENATE INTEREST. RECTIFY PROBLEM. REPORT BY WIRE WHEN YOU READ THIS. FROM W.D. HALLECK. WASHINGTON DC.

Spur growled and stood. He had been planning on taking a day for rest and relaxation there in Denver before he reported in to his Washington slave driver. He could see his plans dissolving.

Ten minutes later he sent a wire to Gen. Halleck reporting he was in Denver and had read the message. He would get to Gold Ledge the next day.

Back at the hotel, he asked the desk clerk for a map of the Colorado Territory. It was a little over 100 miles to Colorado Springs and on to Gold Ridge. Any reputable stage should be able to make that in eight hours. Spur thought of the pounding he'd take bouncing around in a stagecoach, but that was the best way to get there. But he wasn't going anywhere before he got a few hours of shut eye, especially since the stage left at six the next morning.

The next day, after a long but uneventful ride across the territory, Spur wound his long frame out the door of the stage in Gold Ridge. The town was smaller than he figured. Not more than 300 people. He'd heard from the passengers going there that the place was a one-mine town. No ranching, no farming, no timber cutting. Mining was it. When the mine shut down, the whole town would shut down.

It was almost four in the afternoon so Spur headed for the only building in town that could be a hotel. It was. Two floors, 20 rooms, a small dining room, and no hot water for guests. He took a room on the second floor and started to ask the man behind the desk where he could find the Davis house. Then he changed his mind and asked why the hotel had no bathtubs for guests.

The man lifted one brow on his long, thin face. Pimples had pocked one of his cheeks but not the other one, which showed pink and scrubbed clean. His hands fidgeted with the register and he put a key in one of the boxes behind the desk, took it out, and dropped it on the desk. He looked up slowly.

"Now why would you be asking that?"

Spur grabbed the man's shirt and tie an inch below his collar and pulled him against the desk, then forward another six inches.

"Because I want to know. You usually bad-mouth your hotel guests this way? If you want to breathe again, I suggest you tell me instantly why no bathing facilities are available."

Spur's face started to turn red and the clerk nodded. Spur let off the pressure on the twisted shirt and tie, but kept holding them.

"Policy of the hotel. We had a lot of bad experiences with bathing in the rooms. Manager said no more. I don't make policy."

"Good thing," Spur growled and stalked out the front door.

Halfway down the block he stopped a man on the street and asked where he could find the Davis house.

The man frowned, then nodded. "Yep, the widow Davis. She's straight down two blocks on Main, then turn right on that mostly empty block. Hers is the second house of the three that stand in that block."

Spur thanked the man and walked away, figuring the guy would never remember his asking the question. He hadn't decided whether to come in officially here or to play it blind.

Spur McCoy, one of the first Secret Service men appointed by the president, stood two inches over six feet and was coyote slender, cat quick, and expert with all kinds of firearms, explosives, and knives. He also knew a dozen ways to kill a man with his bare hands.

He had cat-green eyes, a clean-shaven face, heavy black brows, long sideburns, and a head full of dark hair, which he let grow a little longer than the usual going-to-church haircut. A master of most horseflesh, he could earn his pay as a cowboy on a ranch, cattle drive, or roundup, and he played poker with the best card sharks in the West, who had taught him most of the common methods of cheating.

He wore clothes suited to the job. Right now he had on range jeans, a dark blue work shirt, a gray leather vest, and a flat-crowned gray Stetson with a flat brim and a string of Mexican silver pesos circling the headband. On his right hip hung a Smith & Wesson .44 centerfire revolver. Hanging low, it was tied down with a leather thong around his lower leg.

Gold Ledge Gold Diggers

Spur walked down the street with a long stride and several men lounging on the boardwalk gave way before him rather than let him go around them. Some watched him pass and stared at his back. Two women in a second-story of the saloon watched him openly and made quick remarks to each other. Both broke up laughing and vanished from the window.

Spur found the second block and turned. He saw the three houses ahead. All looked fairly new; all were of similar style and construction and modest in size. He walked up to the second house on the street and knocked on the door.

The door opened a crack and he saw one dark eye appraising him. "Yes? What do you want?"

"Ma'am, I'm trying to find Charlotte Davis. I don't want to frighten you. I've been sent by the United States government to help you."

There was a moment of silence; then Spur heard a sniffled sob and the door eased open. The woman standing there was only a little over five feet tall with long brown hair, pale soft skin, and delicate features that seemed almost child-like. Her chin quivered and one hand came out slowly.

"You came. Thank the Lord, you came. I prayed for someone to fight these people. They're monsters. They claim to be the town's saviors, but they're monsters thinking only of their own stupid little aims and goals."

She stopped and covered her face with one hand, then lowered it and held it out. "You'll have to excuse my bad manners. I'm Mrs. Charlotte Davis, and I welcome you into my home."

Spur took the hand and felt its softness. She pressed his fingers, then let go.

"Please, come in. We have a lot to talk about. I'll have some tea ready in a few minutes. As you can see, I'm not all that used to having company here in Gold Ledge."

They sat down on chairs that didn't match. The furniture in the living room was basic and sparse. Some of it was handmade and improvised. It was a poor home.

Spur told her how he came to be on her doorstep and she recounted exactly what she had seen the night her husband was lynched.

"There were five of them, Mr. McCoy. One a big, broad-shouldered man taller than the rest. Three were medium size and the fifth was smaller than the others. I couldn't recognize any of the voices because the sound came through their hoods. They didn't have a hole to talk through."

"Anything unusual about the horses?"

"No, just horses, all were dark red or reddish brown, roans or sorrels. No marks or brands that I could see in the dark."

"Not much to go on. Your husband had no enemies in town?"

"No, Lester was a kind, gracious man. He loved everyone. A kinder soul you'll never find. He didn't gamble or stay out. He worked hard every day in the mine. Nobody could fault him."

"So you think he was murdered simply because he was from the South?"

"Yes, the big man said so several times. He said this town didn't need our kind of people. Said we should go back to where we came from. Said he hoped we'd take it as a warning and move on."

Spur frowned. He had hoped there would be some kind of a lead, some clue he could start with. All he had was a general dislike for

Southerners; that inclination was held by probably half the people in the West.

"Who would stand to gain if you left town?" Spur asked.

The small woman shook her head. "I can't think of anyone. We owe no one in town. We pay cash for what we buy. Lester and I saved for six months to build our houses, did most of the work ourselves. We and the other two Southern families are not related but we might as well be. We stay together and we work together. We feel safe and at home with each other."

A knock sounded on the door, which opened a crack. "Charlotte, are you all right?"

Charlotte excused herself and hurried to the front door. A moment later she came into the living room with two women. Both wore cheap calico dresses with white aprons over them. They came to the chairs and Spur was on his feet, holding his hat in his hands.

"Mr. McCoy, I'd like you to meet my two best friends. This is Betty Lou Clinton and Tamara Sue Towers. My neighbors. We're all from Alabama. Their husbands brought my Lester back here that night over three weeks ago so we could bury him."

Spur shook hands with the three women and they all sat down. Betty Lou was sturdy, tall, and well formed. She had a golden mane of hair that had touches of red in it and a friendly face dotted with freckles.

Tamara Sue was barely five feet tall and younger than the others. She had mousy-brown hair and a flat, slightly pinched face; she was thin as a waffle from a hot skillet. She glanced at Spur once, then studied the floor the rest of the visit.

"These ladies have held my world together. If it weren't for them I'd have gone storming downtown with our shotgun and tried to shoot every man in town."

Betty Lou nodded. "She just might have done it, but I hid all of the shotgun shells. Mr. McCoy, is there some way we can get justice for the killing of Lester?"

"I hope so, Mrs. Clinton. Can any of you give me any idea who the five men might be? Have you heard anything around town about a vigilante committee?"

"Oh, they haven't been active for long. They have threatened a few people, run some drunks and riffraff out of town, but to my knowledge this is the first time they have murdered anyone."

"Who runs the town? Do you have a mayor, a city council, or a sheriff?"

"Not much law here," Charlotte said. "We have a deputy from Colorado Springs, where the sheriff is. He's in town three days a week, sometimes four."

"We have a mayor," Mrs. Clinton said. "Or was he appointed? I don't remember."

"Who owns the mine?"

"That's the easy one," Charlotte said. "Nathan R. Havelock. He owns that big house up on the side of the hill. Spends most of his time in Colorado Springs and Denver with the other swells. Don't really pay much attention to business.

"We had a scare about a year ago that the mine was going to close. But it never did. They had lost the vein, but a week later they found it. My Lester said it looked like the vein was petering out again."

Spur stood and paced the room, then looked at the three women. "Ladies, I don't want you to tell anyone who I am or why I'm in town. I'm going to try to smoke out these vigilantes quickly. My plan just might work. Remember, not a word about my being here to anyone, not even to your husbands."

Spur turned toward the door and had it opened when he heard two shots some distance away. Then a dozen more shots came. He waved at the women and ran out of the house. Maybe the vigilantes were at it again and he could catch them in some monstrous act.

Chapter Two

McCoy ran down the street to Main and could see some kind of a gathering half a block ahead. He walked up to the group and saw a man wearing a green shirt with bright red suspenders lift a six-gun toward the sky and fire off three more shots.

"I just had twins!" the man with the revolver shouted. "Twins, you hear, twins!" He fired the hand gun twice more; then a pair of men rushed him into a saloon shouting that he had to buy everyone drinks, and the rest of the crowd cheered and laughed and melted away.

This seemed to be a town where the people lived for the moment, where they expressed their feelings loudly and quickly. McCoy should be able to use that hair-trigger type of mind to get some kind of a lead on the vigilantes. He went to the next bar down the street and pushed his way inside. Two men were coming out and he blocked their way and charged forward bouncing them off both sides of his sturdy shoulders. They slammed into the wall and one fell over a table where a poker game was in session. Both men bellowed in protest but Spur didn't even look back. Instead he swaggered up to the bar and pounded it twice with his fist.

"Whiskey," he brayed and the bartender rushed down with a bottle and a glass. The bartender didn't bother to hold out his hand for the 15 cents. He poured the small glass full and gave it to Spur, who bolted down the shot glass of whiskey in one gulp and slammed the glass down hard.

"Another one," Spur barked and the bartender poured the next shot. Spur lifted it and looked over the glass. "You call this whiskey, son? I've had better whiskey out of a hog trough. Where's the good stuff?"

The bartender pointed to the bottle he held. Spur threw the glass of whiskey in the bartender's face, smashed the glass on the bar, and stalked out of the bar without paying.

He did a similar show in the second saloon in the two-drinking-establishment town. At this one he drew a mild protest from the bartender. Spur snorted and poured that drink down the other man's shirt.

"Pay for the drinks," somebody shouted from a group of a dozen men in the establishment.

Spur spun and drew his six-gun so fast it caused some gasps. Then before anyone could react, he shot out two of the three coal-oil lamps that lit the dim interior of the saloon. Glass shards and kerosene sprayed the men unlucky enough to be in range. Several shouts of protest went up, but no one challenged McCoy. Spur snorted, holstered his Smith & Wesson .44, and glared at the men.

"Don't none of you ever tell me what the hell to do. Understand? Unless you want an early meeting with the undertaker."

McCoy looked around. A small man wearing a business suit stood and started to leave the place. Just as the brown-haired man got to the door he turned and stared at Spur, then hurried out. Spur dropped a 20-dollar double eagle gold piece on the bar and asked for another shot of whiskey. He let it sit on the bar as he studied the men in the room.

It wouldn't take long, he decided. He'd give the messenger 15 minutes. If he'd figured right, the small man in the suit would be running to the powers that ran the vigilante committee and they would make some kind of move. Within 15 minutes they should get into action. Wasn't that what they were supposed to do—police the town and get rid of undesirables?

It took 20 minutes. Spur still stood at the bar nursing his second whiskey. Two big men came in the door and went straight to the bar. Both were taller than Spur and 40 pounds heavier. They wore work clothes and no hats. One had a knife scar across one cheek. The other one had a large bruise over one eye. They walked up on each side of Spur, where he stood facing the bar. They crowded in close against him. Spur stared at them in the mirror behind the bar for only a second.

Spur hesitated no longer. His right elbow slashed upward with the force of a mule's kick, hit the point of the jaw on the man on his right, and blasted him backward into an unconscious heap on the floor.

Almost at the same time, Spur's left hand slashed outward and up. The hard side of his hand jolted into the front of the man's throat with enough force to gag him and send him to his knees, but not hard enough to shatter his windpipe.

Spur watched the suddenly quiet group of saloon birds. One of them turned to the man at his table.

"My God, did you see that? Faster'n blue lightning!"

Spur stepped back, motioned to the two men on the floor. "Somebody drag this trash out into the street and pitch it off the boardwalk." Spur turned and walked out the front door checking out everyone near the entrance.

Two men passing the saloon were of no concern. The small man Spur saw leave the other saloon leaned against the hardware store next door. He smoked a long black cigar. When he saw Spur he dropped the stoggie, turned, and walked away with a try at being casual.

Spur followed him. Ten feet down the boardwalk the small man turned and looked over his shoulder. When he saw Spur tracking him, he ran.

Spur caught him in ten strides, grabbed his arm, jerked him around, and stopped him. Then he walked the short man to the front of a real-estate office and pushed him against the wall.

"Talk," Spur said.

"Let go of me. Why are you chasing me? I got a notion to get the sheriff after you."

The man was two inches over five feet tall. He dressed like a town dandy with his gray suit, vest, and white shirt. The wide knot in his necktie vanished under his vest. His hands were soft and his face white. He wore wire-rimmed eyeglasses, which he pushed high on his nose.

"Talk," Spur said again, this time with a deadly menacing tone that shook the small man.

"I have nothing to talk about. Why should I talk to you?"

"You saw me in the saloon and left. You sent those two idiots in to stop my unruly behavior. What's your name for starters?"

"Odell Vail and I own the real-estate business right behind me. I'm a respected businessman in Gold Ledge. I know nothing about the two ruffians you mention."

As Vail spoke, two men came from the saloon dragging one of the strong-arm men by the shoulders. They dumped him on the boardwalk and looked at Spur. He motioned to the street and they rolled him off the boards into the dirt and horse droppings covering Gold Ledge's main thoroughfare. The second man followed shortly. Spur caught Vail's arm and walked him over to the pair in the gutter.

"Mr. Vail, look closely at these two men. Are you staking your life on the fact that you don't know who they are and that you know nothing about them? If you're lying, you die. Make up your mind in ten seconds."

Vail's eyes went wide and he glanced up and down the boardwalk, but evidently saw no help. He took a deep breath.

"All right, I know them."

"And—"

"And I paid them a dollar each to throw you out of the saloon."

"Now we're getting somewhere. I can have you charged with assault and battery, Mr. Vail, do you know that? Conspiracy to do great bodily harm, as well. You said there's a sheriff in town. Is that true or is he just a deputy?"

"Deputy county sheriff."

"Excellent, Mr. Vail. Let's take a walk to the deputy county sheriff's office. As we go there I'll decide if I want to bring charges against you. Are my intentions precise and clear, Mr. Vail?"

The small man nodded. "Look, I don't know who you are. You created a disturbance in both saloons. We like to run a nice, quiet town here, so I asked those two men to remove you from the saloon before somebody got hurt."

"Just doing your civic duty."

"Exactly."

"Not good enough, Vail. I'll need a lot more reason than that. Are you the mayor or the town marshal?"

"No, sir."

"Then who gave you the authority to take it upon yourself to be the guardian of the town's welfare?"

"My civic duty. Every citizen has to protect the community. Been the law of the West long as I can remember."

"Where were you running to when I caught you?"

"To my office, right here. You scared the hell out of me."

"Did I threaten you?"

"You ran after me."

"Mr. Vail. A warning to you. If you ever send anyone after me again, I'll hunt you down, skin your miserable body slowly, and laugh each time you scream. Do you understand me, Mr. Vail?"

The small man's eyes went wide. He shivered and his hands fumbled at his sides, eventually meeting behind his back and clasping together. His head bobbed. "Oh, yes, sir. I understand. Indeed I do."

"Good, Mr. Vail. Now you enjoy the rest of the afternoon." Spur nodded at the man, who shuffled sideways a step, then two, and hurried to the door of the real-estate-and-land office, which he'd said he owned.

Inside the office, Odell Vail closed the door behind him and leaned heavily against it. Damn him. Damn his eyes for making Odell Vail look foolish in front of half the town. He couldn't let it pass. He simply couldn't let such an affront go unpunished.

What should he do? It could not be a direct confrontation. The gunman had established his credentials both with his physical prowess and with the speed and accuracy of his six-gun. A rifle? Something from long distance? A hired man to do the job? For a moment Vail frowned trying to decide; then slowly he began to smile.

There was a far better way to deal with this man. Yes, he should have known it at once instead of hiring the Batemen brothers to rough him up. Yes, there was a much better solution and it could be handled quickly and efficiently.

Vail frowned for a moment. Would that be too much of a direct tie-in? Dozens of people had seen Vail humiliated. Now if something were to happen to this lout. . . . He needed to think it through. The stranger definitely wasn't the kind of man anyone wanted or needed in Gold Ledge. Not in the slightest.

He would talk about this man tonight. There would be a reaction, and he hoped agreement. As his anger and fear gradually subsided, Vail realized that he had no idea who this man was or why he was in town.

Vail went to the stagecoach office, but Henry behind the counter shook his head. "Sometimes we have names of the passengers, but more often we don't. I don't have any idea who the tall gent is, but he came in from Colorado Springs this noon. I do have names on two of the other passengers, both locals."

Vail thanked Henry and walked out of the stage depot with his quick, measured steps, moving the way he always did, swiftly and with a purpose.

At the hotel, he didn't check the register, instead he talked to the hotel owner in his office off the lobby. Harden Konrad lifted his brows when Vail sat down in the chair beside his desk.

"I'm not looking to buy or sell any property today, Mr. Vail. I don't have any gold-mining claims. So why are you taking up my valuable time?"

"You were snoring when I closed the door, Harden. I need to know who one of your guests is."

"Impossible. We don't give out that information." His sour expression changed and he grinned. "Except to a fellow who can't keep a poker face when he's got a good hand. Which one? Who?"

Vail told him and the owner went out and checked the register. Only two men had signed in that afternoon. One was a regular salesman out of Denver. The other name had to be the tall man with the fast gun.

"Signed in as Spur McCoy. Didn't list any company or home address. We don't require it. Some folks put it down."

Vail scowled as he said the name over to himself three times. It was a trick he had learned to help him remember names. "Spur? What kind of a name is that? Sounds like a cowboy."

"Is he a cowboy?" the hotel man asked.

"How would I know? He doesn't talk like a cowhand." Vail stood, held out his hand, and shook the flabby paw extended to him.

"Thanks, Harden. Anytime I can do you a favor, you give a yell."

Odell Vail walked back to the street and up to his office. He sat behind his desk thinking. Who was this Spur McCoy and why was he in town? Maybe he was a gambler. No, too physical, too good with his six-gun.

Vail felt sweat pop out on his forehead. The stranger had to be a hired gun brought in town by the mine owner, old Nathan R. Havelock. Now why would he want to do that? Vail worried. He dug out a bottle from the bottom drawer of his desk and tipped it, letting the Tennessee sipping whiskey trickle down his throat. It warmed and satisfied him.

It was his thinking medicine. Who else in town could afford to bring in a hired gun with the price tag this man must have? Vail couldn't think of a single one, not with the town nervous and damn near to panic because of stories that the mine was about ready to run out of the gold vein. That would be the end of this town. Real estate would be cheaper than dirt then. Dirt is all it would be—dirt and a few boards that would wither into dust.

Who the hell could hire a fancy gunman if not old Nate R. Havelock? The bastard was always out of town, kicking up his heels and pulling open his fly up there in Denver, or so the story went. His wife had left him for a another man who had ten times Havelock's money. So what else was there for him to do but tomcat around?

That left the mine operation up to the resident manager, Dooley Fairfax. Dooley had been frank the last time he talked with Vail. He'd said not to spread it around, but there was a good chance that the current vein would run out within two weeks. If their efforts to find a new vein didn't pan out within another week, he'd have to suggest to Nate to close down the operation.

Vail put his feet up on his desk and grinned. For a real-estate man he was a little unusual. He didn't own a single piece of land or a building in all of Gold Ledge. He rented this office. He had not loaned any money to anyone to buy property. He had out one personal loan of 100 dollars, but that was not much to lose. His balance in the local office of the Colorado Springs Mountain Bank was never over 100 dollars.

His real money was in the bank in Colorado Springs. He had seen too many boomtowns at mining strikes wither and blow away in an instant. If Gold Ledge went bust, he would be out of there like a rabbit running from a hound dog. And he'd be over 75,000 dollars, richer. It was enough, but he wanted more.

Now what the hell about this damn gunslinger? And who had hired him? Odell Vail pondered the problem as he nipped at the bottle of whiskey again. Damn that was good sipping whiskey.

Dooley Fairfax had been in town on company business when he saw the little drama unfold outside the Deep Shaft Saloon. He saw the Bateman brothers dragged out and rolled in the gutter, and he also saw the big man with the low-tied gun grab Vail. By witnessing those scenes, Fairfax had figured out what had happened. Vail had been playing God again. Damn him. He knew better than that.

Fairfax had decided that he needed a town man inside, and he had considered Vail for the job. He could sit on the property, then buy it up for five cents on the dollar, just to be sure to get the deeds all legal and proper when the town folded. Now Fairfax realized he had to reconsider choosing the little man. Was Vail strong enough for the job? Could he play it straight-faced when he was fooling the people? Fairfax didn't know. But he damn well would find out.

Within a week, Fairfax told himself. Damn, in another week it was going to happen. He'd already sent the letter to Nate R. Havelock. There was no doubt. The vein they were working was petering out faster than he'd thought possible. He figured another week at the most. The eight prospecting tunnels the miners had dug to try to find where the vein continued had not shown a thing.

Fairfax grinned. Old Nate would shrug, say he'd never liked the mine business anyway, take his ten million, and vanish. What the hell did Havelock care? He'd made his pile. Now he could enjoy it. Dooley Fairfax would encourage him to do just that.

He had talked to Nate about the chances of the mine petering out. They had talked over whiskey and two good women one night until exhaustion and morning. Nate agreed that if the place ever went bust, he'd sell the salvage rights to Fairfax for ten dollars, all legal and proper.

Salvage on a mine was hard work, but with some know-how and luck a man could make maybe 2,000 dollars from it. Four years' wages to Fairfax, but a spit in the bucket to Nate R. Havelock.

Fairfax grinned and continued on down the street and to the real-estate office. Fairfax was a tall man and so slender his clothes hung on him as if he had wire hangers for bones. His face was thin almost to gauntness. He wore a soft cloth cap to help hide his balding head, and he kept his hair trimmed short so it didn't stick out.

He had a dozen of the caps, a color to go with each of his six suits, and some to spare. What was left of his hair was a mousy-brown color and so fine it blew in the wind unless he let it stay dirty so it would lie down.

Fairfax had serious blue eyes; his stare could send a miner running for home hoping he wasn't fired the next day. Fairfax lived in a company house halfway up the slope to the mine works. He kept a woman there he had yanked out of the local whorehouse. She had been 16 when he'd found her a year ago. At the time, she'd been so inept, frightened, and ashamed at being a whore that he let his better judgment get shanghaied and he bought her for 200 dollars from Madam Shostach.

Slowly, carefully, gradually he'd introduced the girl to the fine art of making love. He realized she was young and had everything to learn. Who was a better teacher than he? Now she was a delight, a superb lover who took care of his most capricious desires. She was confident, secure, and thankful to him for rescuing her. He knew she figured someday he would marry her, but he never would.

Dooley Fairfax pulled the door open to the real-estate office and stepped inside.

"Dooley, just the man I want to see," Odell Vail said. He rose from his chair and came forward, his hand out.

Fairfax leaped forward and backhanded Vail across the side of the face with a vicious blow that sent the small man stumbling backward, a cry of fear and anger surging from his lips. Vail recovered and backed against the wall, one hand on his face where red welts began to appear.

"Why in hell did you hit me, Fairfax?"

"You stupid bastard of an idiot!" Fairfax brayed. "I'm so furious with you that I can hardly keep from killing you. A good thing I don't have my derringer with me. What in hell were you thinking about when you sent the Batemen brothers after that gunman in the saloon?"

"Is that all you're mad at, Dooley? Hell, he was busting up places, pushing people around, shooting out lamps. I figured it was time we used our power to set him straight."

"You figured? You figured? What the hell did you figure? That here was a man who could be a vicious killer, maybe a hired gun somebody brought in, so you send those two stumble-bum giants in to beat him up? You are pathetic, Vail.

If you had a quarter of a brain you could run for president. I had big plans for you. I was going to make you rich. Now I don't know."

Vail stood by his desk, rubbing the side of his red face and shaking his head. Right then he hated Fairfax with a passion. Why did Fairfax always act as if he knew everything?

"I don't understand, Dooley. How'd I do anything wrong?"

"Anything wrong? The Committee doesn't bother with piddling little things like an obnoxious drunk. We reserve our power and our decisions for larger, more important things. We do something that will be a service to the community. Remember that family of Indians we ran out of town two months ago? That was a service to the town of Gold Ledge."

"Oh, and the Southern guy Davis," Vail said, his eyes shining. "We hung his ass high up in that oak tree to help the town, right, Dooley?"

"Yes, Vail. Maybe you're getting the idea. We don't bother with riffraff in the saloons. The problem is what you did might make somebody think it was in some way connected to the Committee. If that were true, then this man you tried to discipline will watch you like a hawk and follow you to try to get some information about our Committee. We can't allow that to happen. What if he came to town trying to find out who we are? We've made some noise. Somebody might not like us doing it, so they sent in some gunman to look for us. He went around trying to get noticed, just hoping somehow we would tip our hand. He was baiting us, almost asking us to challenge him and knock him down a peg. If we did that we might be letting him know we were part of the Committee. That's exactly what you damn well might have done."

"Oh, damn," Vail said. "I just never thought about that. I'll be careful from now on. I know him. If I see him following me I won't talk to anybody. Maybe you shouldn't even be here."

"I was discreet coming in, Vail. I'm not an idiot. I'll go out the back door. You're the son of a bitch I'm worried about. I don't want you doing anything without approval of every man in the Committee. You understand me?"

"Yeah, sure, Dooley. Just don't get so mad. Hell, we're the ones doing the good things here. I just figured—"

"Don't figure anything else. Let people with at least half a brain do the thinking. Now do we have this damn straight?"

"Yeah, Dooley, sure. I just don't like you calling me stupid all the time."

Dooley Fairfax snorted. "Then don't keep on doing stupid things. Now, I got to get out of here. I came to town for some blasting caps. We ran out up at the mine. Never seen a mine run out of dynamite or blasting caps before, but we damn well did. Now what we have to do is figure out what to do next."

"Not sure I understand," Vail said.

"Good, you're asking questions. What we need now is another small strike by the Committee so nobody thinks we're just against the damn Rebs."

"Like the Indian family?"

"Right, but we're out of Indians."

"How about that cheating gambler you complained about. What's his name? Bottom Jenkins?"

Gold Ledge Gold Diggers

Fairfax grinned and sat on the edge of the desk. "Now that's a damn good idea. Bottom Jenkins took me for almost two hundred dollars. I owe him. He cheats. Everybody knows he cheats. We'll have a meeting of the Committee tonight and work out the details. Meet at my house up toward the mine at midnight. Just be sure to come. Yes, Vail, damn good idea. We'll set it up for tomorrow morning sometime, soon as the damn gambler has his breakfast."

Vail beamed at the approval. "What you expect we might do to this gambler guy?"

"The Committee will decide, but I'm partial to hot tar and two pillows full of chicken feathers."

"Oh, damn, but that sounds fine," Vail shouted. Both men were grinning when Fairfax stepped out the rear door of the real-estate office into the alley.

When the door to the alley closed, Odell Vail walked back to his desk smiling. He had been enthusiastic about the Committee ever since Fairfax had suggested it six months earlier. The Committee hadn't done much, but it served a real purpose. They had run two families out of town, the Indian and some riffraff who wouldn't work and stole anything they found loose. Then they had hung the damn Rebel. Vail had been reluctant to do it, but when the rest of them told the horror stories about what the Rebels had done to Northern prisoners, he changed his vote to a yes.

Now Fairfax had liked his idea about going after the gambler. Oh, yes, it would be great sport and the man wouldn't be hurt too badly. Vail would take pains to be sure the tar would stick, but not burn the man. He grinned again and sat behind his desk, his feet on the first drawer and his fingers locked together in back of his head.

Chapter Three

After his run-in with Odell Vail, Spur went from the real-estate office across the street to the general store and asked the clerk for some .44 solid cartridges. The clerk handed over the box of 30 and motioned to Spur's six-gun.

"You use 'em, huh?" the man asked. "We ain't seen many of them new-fangled weapons around here."

"Get used to them. The solid cartridges are the ammunition of the future. All of the percussion six-guns can be converted to solid rounds. Lots faster to load. I've seen a man fire solid loads when his whole piece was underwater crossing a river. Came out and fired just fine. You'll never see a ball-and-cap weapon shoot after a good dunking."

"Damn you say!" the young man shook his

head. "How fast can you reload? I guess that's a big advantage."

Spur nodded. "With a little practice a man can reload six rounds in ten to twelve seconds. You know how long it takes to reload with the percussion cap-and-ball weapons."

They talked six-guns awhile and Spur showed the kid the Smith and Wesson .44, but didn't let him hold it. "I never give up my weapon to anybody."

Afterward, McCoy went down the block to the Golden Goose Cafe. It didn't serve roast goose. He found a place to sit and ordered an early dinner—steak and a couple of side dishes.

Spur enjoyed the meal and had just finished when a woman walked in. She had dark hair around her shoulders; her bangs were cut across her forehead. The black hair framed a pert, pretty face that had a touch of the Oriental about it. He watched her sit down and saw a slice of slender ankle. His gaze met hers for just a second; then she looked away.

Spur grinned, picked up his coffee cup, and walked over to the table where she sat. He cleared his throat and she looked up.

"Miss, someone spilled coffee on my chair and since it's so crowded in here, I wondered if you'd mind if I shared your table?"

She looked up with wide-set green eyes that startled him. Her face was cold and distant; high cheekbones mocked him. She turned her head, sending her long dark hair in a swirl of jet radiance. Then she looked around at the nearly empty cafe and smiled.

"It does seem to be crowded, doesn't it? You're a stranger in town, so it would be impolite of me to refuse. Please sit down."

Gold Ledge Gold Diggers

Her voice had a belllike quality to it that Spur had never heard before. He sat and saw that her dress was not country calico, but a finely woven and cut princess type that accented her slender waist and showed off her rising bosom.

She smiled at him. "Did I pass inspection?"

"Delightfully. I'm sorry, I didn't mean to stare, but I never expect to find a beautiful woman like you in a little mining town out here in the back country wilds of Colorado."

"Well, aren't you diplomatic and nice?" She smiled again and held out her hand. "So we can be formally introduced, I'm Gwen Havelock. I own a women's wear store here in town. The only one. Since you're new in Gold Ledge, I'll tell you that I'm the daughter of the owner of the gold mine up the hill. I wanted something to do, and I've always enjoyed fine clothes. So I hired a seamstress and have my own dress shop. I love it."

"I'm impressed and happy to meet you, Miss Havelock. Yes, I am new in town. I'm Spur McCoy. I'm here on business."

She raised a brow. "But the only businesses in town are mining and catering to the mine employees."

"That's one of the big problems of boomtowns near mines," Spur said. "I've seen towns mushroom around placer mining strikes. The placer gold lasts six months, and the town is gone a week after the gold dust is all dug out."

"That won't happen here. The mine should be good for five years yet. By then we should have ranchers who can run cattle in some of the high valleys. That and a stage line will help us build a stable community."

Spur smiled. "I'd say you're dreaming some fantasy, but it looks like you really love this little town."

"I do. My business is here. If the mine shuts down, the town goes with it, and my business as well."

"You could always move to Colorado Springs or on to Denver."

"Wouldn't be the same."

"True. Oh, are you having dinner?"

"Just coffee."

"Your father must have a big house here."

She smiled. "Yes, he built it the first year. This is my third year here. Father moved to Denver two years ago and now only comes back once in a while. I rattle around the place."

A waitress brought Gwen coffee and refilled Spur's cup. He settled back and watched the beautiful girl. He guessed she was about 22, maybe a year more. Good school, probably a year in Europe. He admired the way her breasts rode high in her chest and pressed out on the fabric.

"What kind of business are you in, Mr. McCoy?"

"Real estate. I buy for a Denver outfit, if I can find the right property at the right price."

"Don't buy here." She blurted her words out; then she frowned and looked down at her hands, which she had folded in her lap.

Spur kept his poker face on and rubbed his chin. "Which must mean you know something that most of the others here in town don't. Is the mine playing out?"

She looked around quickly and saw that there was no one near them who could hear.

"Don't say that, Mr. McCoy. Don't even think

it. My whole future is wrapped up in this town. I don't want to move to Denver."

"So there is something to this mine closing rumor."

"I really can't say anything about that." She looked up, her somber eyes pleading with him. "Please, we must talk about something else."

"Fine. Is there a theatre in town, a traveling acting troupe, even a symphony orchestra?"

She smiled and he smiled, caught up in the glow. "I'm afraid not. We're too far off the well-trodden path for the companies to come here. They'd go broke. Our miners don't enjoy Shakespeare."

"But I bet you do, Gwen."

She looked up when he used her first name. Then she nodded. "Yes, I do. I've seen seven of his plays. I've forgotten how many he wrote, thirty-two, I think." She watched him from behind a soft smile. "You must know something of the Bard too."

"I saw some performances in Boston."

Her eyes flared with interest. "Boston? Oh, I've always wanted to go there."

"Interesting, but a long way away. How can I take you to a play if there isn't one on the boards here?"

"I'm afraid you can't."

"We could go for a walk."

"Two blocks up and two blocks back," she said. Then she smiled and her lips pulled back showing perfect white teeth. "A small idea, if you don't think it's too forward of me. Do you play chess?"

Twenty minutes later she ushered him into the living room of the three-story Havelock mansion

41

built on the hillside over the town but not all the way up to the mine. It was far enough away so the constant thumping of the stamping mill didn't penetrate the double-wall construction.

"My castle," Gwen said. "Yes, I have help here and at the store. I'm there most of the time, but this week there has been almost no business. That damn rumor about the mine closing started a week ago and now no one is buying anything. All of the merchants are on edge. I just hope the town doesn't explode."

A small Chinese woman came into the living room and bowed.

"Ling How, this is Mr. McCoy. I think we would like some hot tea and some of those small sweet cakes you made this morning. We'll be playing chess in the library."

Spur admired the sleek, slender form of the Chinese girl. Her dress outlined her body within a quarter of an inch of reality. He looked back at Gwen, who had seen his appraising glance.

"She's amazing, isn't she? So efficient, so loyal, and so attractive. But it's a package that you are not to open." Gwen grinned at his surprised look and led him through the living room.

They stopped in the library. The walls were crowded with several bookcases, each with its own glass door.

"The doors keep the books from gathering dust," Gwen said. "Father has some valuable first editions here. He's always planned to move them to Denver, but since Mother left him, he just hasn't had the gumption to do it."

One window overlooked the downward slope and they could see the whole town of Gold Ledge below them. Gwen took out a hand-carved set of ivory chessmen and arranged them on the board.

"Black or white?" she asked and the game began.

Spur started with his best opening gambit, but she blocked him in the traditional way and began a series of daring offensive thrusts against his king.

The tea and small sweet cakes came and they worked on them between moves. Gwen made the first mistake by not spotting the damage Spur's knight could do. He quickly traded her queen for his knight and after that it was 12 moves until he had checkmate.

"Another game," Gwen said.

"You don't like to lose," Spur said. "Or did you simply give me the game to be a good hostess."

She looked up, her green eyes sending off angry sparks. "I've never thrown a game of chess in my life. I certainly won't start losing on purpose now to some upstart gunslinger from Boston."

The sparks eased down to glowing coals of green fire. "I heard about your little fracas in the saloon this afternoon. Poor Mr. Vail was mortified. I wouldn't be surprised if he tried to get his revenge against you."

"A lot better men than Vail have tried but I'm still alive and kicking."

"Alive and shooting would be a better choice of words," Gwen said. She paused in setting up the chessboard. "Do you really want to play another game?"

"Not of chess."

Gwen smiled and pushed aside the board and moved around to the softness of the sofa, where

Spur sat. "What kind of game did you have in mind?"

She sat close to him and Spur bent slowly and kissed the side of her neck. He kissed her again and again up to the point of her jaw and around to her lips. He paused as he leaned in to let his lips touch hers. Gwen whimpered softly as their lips met. Then her hands went to his head and held him as the kiss stretched out.

When it ended she moved away from him so she could see him better.

"That kind of game," Spur said. "I'd bet that you've played before."

"We don't have to keep score?"

"Never keep score. It's how well you play the game that counts."

Gwen laughed softly. "I like strong men. When I heard how easily you handled the two Batemen brothers, I guessed you might be somebody I'd want to meet. My father is a weakling. He let mother run all over him. That's why she ran away and took half of his money."

She leaned in and kissed his lips hard and demanding, holding the back of his head with her hand and brushing his lips with her tongue. She ended the kiss and moved away and stood.

"We have a much better game room upstairs." She held out her hand for him. He took it, stood, and pulled her forward, picking her up in his arms. Gwen laughed softly. "Oh, yes, I think this is going to be a remarkably good game."

She directed him up an open staircase and down a hall on the second floor. It looked like a guest bedroom. A large canopied bed was set near the window so the lights of the small town below could be seen. Spur was surprised that it was dusk. He lit two lamps with heavy shades and cut-crystal decorations.

Gwen looked at him, then brought in two more coal-oil lamps, and lit them, making the room almost daylight bright.

"I always like to see what I'm doing," Gwen said. "It doesn't matter what game it is I'm playing."

She sat down on the edge of the bed and looked at the empty spot beside her. Spur sat close so his leg touched hers under the sleek dress from her hip down to her calf.

"No fair cheating," Gwen said.

Spur leaned away in exaggerated surprise. "Young lady, this is the only game in the universe where neither of the parties are capable of cheating. Everything must come from the heart. This is the game where we both lay bare our souls and for a few moments the truth, even if unwelcome, is laid naked for both of us to see."

Gwen frowned. "Oh, damn. I don't know all the rules. Maybe I don't want to play this game with you."

"Maybe," Spur said.

Then he took her in his arms and kissed her lips hotly, his tongue darting against her lips until she opened them and let him stab inside her. She battled him a moment, then gave in with a small sigh.

When the kiss ended, Spur leaned back and watched the pretty lady. Her eyes went wide, her nostrils flared for a moment, and her mouth came open as she panted.

"My God, but that was exciting," Gwen said. "I like this part of the game."

Spur kissed her again and this time pulled her

backward on the bed until she lay on top of him. Their lips were fused together. Spur felt his own blood heating, rising, filling him with the age-old need to have this woman. The kiss ended and Gwen pushed up until she sat on his hips staring down at him.

"I like it up here," she said and grinned. "It gives me a feeling of power, as if I could make you do anything I want you to. Right now, I'll give you one guess what it is I want you to do."

She undid some hidden fasteners on the bodice of her dress. Then pulled the dress off her shoulders and down until both breasts came into view. Her breasts were not huge, but they tipped upward with rose areolas and dark-tipped nipples.

"You know what I want to do?" Spur asked. He reached up and boosted Gwen onto his torso, then brought her down until one of her breasts hung delightfully over his mouth. "May I have the honor?"

"If you don't I'll shoot you dead," she said and lowered the breast into his open mouth.

He watched her face as he sucked on the half globe, then teased it and nibbled on her nipple. He could feel it grow and harden in his mouth. Her eyes went wide with delight. Then her smile sweetened and a faraway look came over her and she began to sing a little ditty that Spur didn't recognize. He moved his ministrations to her other breast and her look of total rapture continued.

When he finished nibbling at her second nipple he lifted her away, and she bent and kissed his lips so hard it hurt him. She left him quickly and slid off him to begin unbuttoning his pants.

"Now it's my turn to chew on you a little," she

said. Gwen shivered as she worked through his pants and underwear and soon pulled his erection from the restraining cloth.

"Oh, my!" she said softly, then bent and kissed him from his roots right out to the pointed purple head of his pulsating erection.

"My, what a fine big boy," she said and slowly inched his penis into her open mouth. A moment later she began to bob up and down on him and Spur had to reach down and stop her. She looked up, an impish smile on her face. "This way later?" she asked.

He nodded and worked at undressing her. She helped him. Soon both of them were naked and lying on the bed face-to-face, not touching, just watching each other and looking at their bodies.

"You're so perfect," she trilled. "Such wide, strong shoulders and heavily muscled arms but with a slender torso and waist. Not much hips but powerful legs and strong feet. A man is a true work of art. I wish I were an artist so I could paint you nude doing all sorts of different things."

"What would you have me do first?" Spur asked, enjoying her description of him.

She rolled on top of him, pushing him flat on his back and kissing him hard. "Do me good and hard, Spur McCoy. Stick your spur inside me and make me see stars right inside this room."

Her excitement and enthusiasm caught him and pulled him along. He lifted her and she moved down, then adjusted her hips a moment and picked up his erection and lowered herself gently onto his shaft. They fit together perfectly.

"Oh, my!" Gwen said. She trembled and gasped, and before he could do more than hold her with both arms, she tore into a strong climax that shook both of them, twisted her pretty face, and sent her hips steam hammering at his hips until Spur thought he would lose control.

She finished and gave a long sigh and opened her eyes. "You are magic, Spur McCoy. I've never come that way before. You are a miracle worker, a true wonder. I want to lock you in the attic and bring you out twice a day to service me and keep you all to myself for as long as we can make love."

They both chuckled. Then Spur lifted her hips to give him some room and he began punching into her slowly at first, then faster and faster. She caught the rhythm and maintained the motion, riding him like a range bull with its front feet up on the back of a virgin heifer on the open range.

Gwen exploded first, smashing into a million pieces and raining down on the room like snow flakes—only to fly together and glue themselves once more into a pretty naked lady jolting and lunging and whimpering and letting out a wild, high-pitched keening that echoed through the whole house.

She came down slowly and Spur waited for her. When her eyes opened and she looked at him, Spur began his trip to paradise. He drove upward into her willing den again and again until she caught at him with her inside muscles milking him on every stroke.

Soon he tore himself apart with a series of jolting ejaculations that scattered his body over six states and never did bring him back together. He struggled to open his eyes and found himself magically restored. Gwen kissed his feverish brow and whispering words of love and adoration in his ear.

"Oh, damn," Spur managed to utter. "You damn near killed me. How come you're so good at making love?"

She ground her hips against him, pushing him against the feather mattress. "Just lucky, I guess. Comes with good genes. My old daddy is the biggest fucker in Denver. He's had the best parts of half the rich women in that city."

Spur grinned. "He sure did fine putting you together. I'll say that for the old man."

Gwen eased off him and they lay on the bed side by side, whispering and talking about nothing at all. Then she sat up and frowned down at him.

"Now I see why you're in town. You came to buy the mine. You think you can take it over. Even though my daddy thinks it's about played out, you think you can turn it into a money-making hole in the ground again."

"Not a chance. I don't have that kind of money, and I know nothing about mining or stamping or recovering the pure gold. It's all a mystery to me."

"Then why are you in a little burg like this?"

Spur McCoy told her who he was and why he was there. "These vigilantes wouldn't have rated our attention if it wasn't the blatant murder of a Southerner. The federal government is starting to bend over backward to strike down on this intolerance situation in the West. My job to see that it happens. Are you disappointed in the real me?"

Her brows rose and she caught his hands and pulled them over her breasts. "Oh, no. Just the opposite. The idea that you're a federal lawman gets my little crotch twitching just ever so fast. It makes me want you more than ever. I'm getting goose bumps right now just dreaming about how we're going to fuck the next time. You have any suggestions?"

He did. Before the night was over six of the suggestions turned out to be the right ones. They got to sleep just as dawn shattered the night's hold on the eastern peaks and the roosters crowed in the village of Gold Ledge.

Chapter Four

The morning after the Fairfax-Vail meeting, and after Spur and Gwen's tempestuous night in bed, McCoy and Gwen had a big breakfast a little after seven o'clock. Gwen kept touching Spur's hand and his arm and his shoulders. She shook her head.

"I am amazed. I'm not a wide-eyed virgin who just had her first sexual experience, but I can't keep from touching you. We really did well together and I loved it. Do you know that?"

"We were fine, better than fine. Maybe we can arrange to try it again one of these nights?"

"If you don't come back to my bed and stay the night, I just might track you down and shoot you dead myself."

They both laughed. The small Chinese girl had fixed a huge breakfast for them. Spur found out that Ling How was 18 but he swore she was a lot younger. Gwen had to get to the shop to supervise a woman's dress fitting that morning. Spur wanted to get up to the mine to talk to the resident manager and find out what the dead man's job had been to see if the position had had anything to do with his death.

First he would talk to the widow again, to see if she knew anything about what her husband had been doing at the mine. There was little chance it would prove anything, but at this point, Spur had to dig into every angle of the man's life.

Spur had tangled with vigilante groups before. Often they were started in a town or community where there was little local law or the law was corrupt. Many times the most outstanding men in the area were leaders of the groups. But over time the upstanding men often left the vigilante committees. The people in them changed and sometimes they developed into criminal elements that acted to the detriment of everyone else in town.

Such a group had operated in Missouri back a few years in Short Falls. They were known as the Bald Knobbers and terrorized the town and the whole area with their own brand of justice. He hoped he could nip this vigilante group in its infancy before it grew into a monster.

Spur and the mine owner's daughter decided to leave the house at different times.

"I still have a good reputation in this town and I don't want it shattered just yet, even for you, McCoy," Gwen said. "We can be discreet. I'll go out the front door and you use the back way. It leads down a trail to the other end of Main Street. No one will be any wiser."

"Except Ling How."

Gold Ledge Gold Diggers

Gwen laughed softly, kissed Spur on the lips, and smoothed the hair off his forehead. "She knows my every move. Perhaps the next time she can join us in our games."

"Both of you?"

"Sure, I don't mind sharing." Gwen reached up and kissed Spur hotly, then left with great reluctance and walked out the front door. Spur hurried out the back entrance and down the trail to the end of Main Street.

Spur spent two hours watching the real-estate office, hoping to follow the small real-estate man, but Vail didn't come to his office. Spur changed plans and five minutes later he knocked on the widow Davis's front door. It opened a crack. Then he heard a sigh of relief and the door swung in all the way.

"Oh, Mr. McCoy. I never know who is coming to my door. Sometimes it frightens me."

"That's what I'm here to take care of, Mrs. Davis. Could I come in and talk with you for a few minutes?"

She said he could and he asked the questions about her husband's work just before he was killed.

"No, he didn't say much about it. He did tell me that he and another man were on a kind of special project but he didn't explain it. He said he was told not to talk about it to anyone at the mine or in town."

"Did he sound excited about it or bored? Or was it just another job he did to earn his pay?"

"He was excited about it. About a week before he died, he was just busting to talk about something but he grinned and shook his head and kissed me and said he promised that he would tell no one, not even me. That was the last he talked about it."

"Was he happy that last week?"

"Oh, he was. There had been rumors about the mine closing. He had been concerned about that for a while, but I don't remember him worrying any about it that last week. Is this going to help you find out who those vigilantes are?"

"I hope so, Mrs. Davis. It just might. I have to find out as much about your husband as I can. Oh, was he on this project alone? Or were there other miners involved?"

"He did say something about that right at first. He said there were twelve of them, but he just worked with one other man on his own project. That's all he talked about it to me."

Charlotte Davis watched this strange, tall man who was so intent on finding out about her husband. He was interesting and appealing, but she would never let him know she thought so. For just a moment she wondered what his slender hips would look like without his clothes. She lifted her brows, then frowned slightly. It had only been a month or so since she'd had a man. She wasn't that hard up. Still, he was interesting. She shook her head to rattle out the fantasy.

"Is it important what Lester did at the mine? If it is I could—"

McCoy held up his hand. "Ma'am, I'm just kind of scratching at anything I think might itch here. Grasping at straws. I need to find out everything I can about your husband, so I can run down that one little fact that will help me dig out the men who took his life. If you recall anything he might have said about his work, no matter how small or seemingly unimportant, you write it down and tell me."

"Yes, sir, Mr. McCoy, I most certainly will. I won't rest a single night until the men who did that awful thing to Lester are put away good and proper."

"That's what we hope we're going to do, Mrs. Davis. Now I better be getting downtown so I can find the man I need to talk to." Spur touched his hat, then walked out the front door and along the dusty street.

The man he wanted to find, real-estate agent Odell Vail, still hadn't come to his place of business this morning. Either that or he had come when Spur had been talking to Mrs. Davis. McCoy tried the handle and found the office door locked, as before. Spur heaved a disappointed sigh and walked over to the hardware store across the street. He sat in one of the wooden-frame chairs placed outside for the convenience of the townsmen. Spur lowered himself into the chair and had just made contact with the seat when a voice snapped at him.

"That'll be two bits rent, you young whipper-snapper."

Spur looked to his right, where he saw a dried-up old prune of a man with bones pushing hard against his yellowed skin wherever they showed. The old-timer was hatless. Wisps of his straggling white hair were pasted to his tanned skull and his sunken eyes glared at Spur.

"These is jist for members. You a member of the eighty-year club? Figured as how not. Get up and move on. Pay up or move on, I say, or I'll have the law on you."

Spur chuckled, fished a quarter out of his pocket, and tossed it toward the old codger. The man saw it coming and made a stab at it and missed. A small boy sitting near by pounced on the coin and streaked away down the street as the man screeched at him with a string of swear words that would make a seaman grin in admiration.

The old man looked back. "Well, you paid. Sit a spell. Been in town long? Guess not. Everybody else ignores me when I demand my two bits. Just a few strangers fall for it. Oh, hell, nothing else to do around here. No good-looking women to stare at."

Spur chuckled and leaned back in the solid chair until the high back touched against the side of the store. He let out a long sigh and was about to say something to the old man when two shots sounded down the way and a strange little parade came onto Main from a side street. Two men on horses led the parade. Both the riders wore white hoods.

Spur dropped the chair forward and raced down the boardwalk toward the hooded riders. Behind them came two men with a pole on their shoulders. Tied to the pole by his hands and feet was a human form, tarred black by some brush and then powdered with feathers. Only his face escaped the treatment. The men carrying the pole were big and wore no hoods. A moment later Spur realized they were the brothers he had tangled with when he'd first hit town.

Spur ran another 50 feet to come abreast of the little parade. He had his six-gun out and fired a shot into the air. The hurrahing stopped, and in the sudden silence, the ominous click of Spur's gun hammer cocking drilled through the void.

"You men with the pole, let the poor soul down," Spur bellowed. One of the hooded men snarled and looked at Spur. The hooded man dug for his six-gun but Spur changed his aim and shot his horse in the head.

The animal went down as if it had been hit by lightning. The rider tried to jump off the mount. Instead he ended up sprawled in the dirt of the street. Finally he scrambled to his feet and sprinted for the closest store on the other side of the street. Another hooded figure had spurred his mount forward the moment the second shot came from Spur and his big roan was 30 feet down the street before Spur turned his attention that way.

"Let him down," Spur said again. His words had the snap and steel of authority in them.

No hooded riders followed the tarred-and-feathered man. Slowly the Batemen brothers let the pole down until the man touched the dusty street. Then they ran across Main and bolted into a store.

Spur and half-a-dozen other men rushed to the aid of the tarred man.

"Tar warn't scalding hot," one of the men said. "Don't look like he got burned much."

Another man cut the victim from the pole. Spur saw that the tarred man was naked and his genitals had been generously covered with the tar and feathers.

"Who is he?" Spur asked.

"Bottom Jenkins," another man said. "A gambler. Got the nickname 'cause he dealt from the bottom so much. He got caught so often he shifted his cheating to other ways. The name stuck and he couldn't shake it."

"Get him cleaned up," Spur ordered. "Here's two dollars for kerosene and some towels. Better do it soon and then take him to the doctor. You have one in town?"

"Yeah, Doc Gaylord."

"Get to it," Spur said again and two men came out of the group and helped the tarred man to hobble down the street.

Spur went to look at the dead horse. Two men had attached ropes to the animal's front legs and were about to drag it out of the street. Spur held up his hand and stopped them. The animal had no brand. He checked the saddle. Burned into the saddle he saw the brand of the local livery.

Spur turned and walked toward the far end of town, where he had seen the livery barn and stables. He had no idea who owned the place. When he got there he found a boy in his teens pitching hay into mangers for the stabled animals.

"Who's in charge?" Spur asked.

The kid stopped forking the hay and pointed at a small room built into the side of the barn. "Be Mr. Yale over yonder."

"You rent a couple of horses in the last hour?" Spur asked.

"I don't rent. I use the fork."

Spur pushed open the office door and saw a man sitting at a battered desk, bent forward and sleeping on his arms.

"Are you Yale?" Spur asked, but the man didn't move. "Rise and shine, Yale. It's morning!"

Still the man didn't move. Spur stepped forward and lifted the man's head by his hair. His eyes were closed and a trickle of vomit showed down his chin and into a thick, matted beard. The man was passed out drunk and must have been that way for hours.

The vigilantes had covered their tracks well. McCoy should have shot them both out of their saddles. Next time he would—if there was a next time. From now on the vigilantes would be coming after him. And he would be ready.

Spur went down Main to the first cross street, walked to the alley, and cut back through the alley the way he had come. He found the back door to the dress shop and slipped inside when no one was looking. He went to the back room and then to the door that led to the front.

Twice Spur called softly to Gwen. She heard him the second time and made an excuse to go into the storeroom. Once inside, she pushed a wooden bolt and locked the door.

"I heard what happened out there on the street. That man they tarred and feathered—it was just awful." Her sweet face was shrouded with fear and worry. "Will that get you into trouble with the vigilantes?"

"Yes. Maybe that way I can find out who they are. When I do, I'll arrest them for the murder of Lester Davis."

"But isn't it dangerous? Won't they be trying to kill you now?"

"More than one man has tried that."

She put her arms around him and held him tight. "Be careful. I don't want anything to happen to you. Don't stay at the hotel tonight. You'll be an easy target there. Stay with me. I'll let you sleep all night and won't touch you so you'll be strong and ready for anything tomorrow. Will you come?"

Spur nodded. "I'll come, but I may be late. I want to roam the town, watching and waiting for them to try something. I won't make myself an easy target, but they'll never make a play if I hole up at your house all the time. You understand?"

A tear seeped out of the corner of her green eyes. She brushed it away and nodded, then she kissed him. He eased away from her and reloaded his six-gun. He couldn't believe that he'd walked halfway through town with only three live rounds. He slid in three to fill all the cylinders, marveled again at how easy it was to load the new solid cartridges, and pecked the pretty lady's lips.

"I'll be at the back door by midnight," Spur said, then slipped out through the rear room and into the alley. It wasn't noon yet. He had a lot of time to make himself a target.

Chapter Five

Poker Alice sat in the Deep Shaft Saloon at the back card table that had its own kerosene lamp hanging overhead; she stared at her hand of five-card draw. Not the best. But that had never stopped her before. She studied her cards and leaned forward to tap a chip on the tabletop.

She let the white blouse she wore sag a little forward and then a little more, revealing the hard line of cleavage showing between milky white breasts.

Poker Alice knew the effect on the four men around the table. All had been watching her small flash of flesh, not thinking about their cards. She planned it that way. A little tit could win more hands than an ace up her sleeve. She deftly slipped two cards out of her hand and dropped them onto the table. She held a jack of diamonds, a queen of hearts, and a six of spades.

"Two cards," she said to the dealer, who had almost let his eyeballs pop out of their sockets as he stretched taller to try to see farther down her blouse.

"Uh, yeah, right. Phil, you in the game? Cards?" They went around the table. Three men took three cards, the dealer took two, and Alice accepted her twin pasteboards.

Poker Alice was a small woman, an inch over five feet, with soft brown hair that she kept cut short so it was easy to care for. She wore expensive dresses that she bought in New York City.

She had stormed into Gold Ledge a week earlier, and bystanders guessed so far she had won over 1,000 dollars in her gambling games. She played at any time of the day and had been seen starting a game one afternoon and playing through to the next day at noon. She had won the last pot that day when the two men left in the game folded.

Poker Alice lit another fat, black cigar and blew a cloud of blue smoke into the pot. Her hand was bad, a pair of jacks. The dealer had opened with at least a pair of jacks. She tapped the ash off her cigar and put the cigar back in her face. Her right eye squinted as smoke from the stogie drifted into it.

"Opener bets," Alice said. The dealer stared at her, shrugged, and threw a five dollar chip into the pot. One man dropped out. Alice did the five and raised the man ten. She suddenly found a great interest in her fingernails on her left hand and bent over the table to stare closely at her fingers.

The movement surged her large breasts higher and sagged her blouse open more until the two men across from her could see a sizable portion of her breasts, including the twin arcs of soft pink areolas.

The dealer stared. Poker Alice looked up at him. "Pete, it's ten dollars to you if you're still playing."

The dealer lifted his brows and, without checking his cards, threw in a ten dollar chip. Another player dropped out and the third one still in saw the raise and raised Alice five dollars.

She grinned, straightened up, and absently rubbed her breast. Then she nodded. "See your five and raise you twenty." The only other two players still in the hand folded and she won the pot without showing her cards.

Alice puffed on the stogie without the trace of a smile on her face. She grinned inside. Damn, if she hadn't bluffed them again. It was her deal. She had been watching the men play and had not seen anyone cheating. No bottom dealing or machines up sleeves to produce a winning hand out of the blue.

Before she dealt, she reached into her reticule and took out a sleek little .45 derringer. She cocked the hammer and lay the weapon on the poker table beside her right hand. Two of the players gaped at the gun in surprise.

"Damn, Alice, you don't need no hideout in this game," one of the men said.

"Let's make damn sure," Poker Alice said. "See that frame around that picture down there behind the bar?" The picture was 35 feet away. "Watch the right-hand side of the frame in the middle." Alice's right hand lifted the derringer off the table and in one continuous move she swung up the little two-shot pistol and fired.

The .45 slug dug a hole through the right side of the inch-wide picture frame. Alice pulled out the spent round and put in a fresh one. Then she reloaded the derringer and put it back on the table beside her.

"New dealer, new deck of cards. It's five-card stud. Let's see what kind of nerve you gents have."

Poker Alice had made a name for herself in the West. She played gut-hard poker, never cheated, and didn't tolerate anyone who did. More than one cheater had a new bullet hole in his shoulder and sometimes his right hand from her derringer to prove her anger about cheating.

She was somewhere around 35 when she stopped by Gold Ledge. Her brown hair was still attractive and her face too small and round to be beautiful, but she was often described as cute because she had dimples dotting both cheeks and flashing brown eyes that had tricked more than one man into folding when he had the winning hand.

She had buried two husbands, left a third, and seemingly had no thought to wed again. She did have one ambition, though that was unfulfilled. She wanted to own a big ranch and a gold mine.

"Any of you gents own the gold mine up the hill? I've always wanted to play one hand of poker for a gold mine, or maybe cut for high card for an operating gold diggings. Maybe next time."

A man stepped out of the ring of onlookers who had been watching the famous Poker Alice playing and introduced himself.

"Miss Alice, I don't own the gold mine, but I'm Dooley Fairfax, the general manager of the Gold

Ledge Number One gold mine, maybe I could get in the game, seeing you only have five players."

"You have the deed to the mine on yer person?" Poker Alice asked.

"I'm afraid not."

"Then you have any cash money you want to lose?"

"Would fifty dollars be enough?"

Poker Alice waved the butt of her black cigar at him. "Hell, every fifty dollars helps. Sit down. Welcome the new sucker, guys. Now, are we playing poker or conducting a discussion group here?"

The game lasted for two hours. Fairfax was a better poker player than Alice had expected. He won several pots and even outbluffed her once. Still she wound up ahead by about 300 dollars. Fairfax doubled his 50 dollars and looked satisfied.

"Buy you dinner?" he asked Poker Alice.

"Why?"

"I have a business proposition for you."

"That's not the only kind of propositions that I enjoy. Where are we eating?"

An hour later at the Colorado Cafe, Fairfax and Poker Alice leaned back and lit up after-dinner cigars.

"What I want you to do is to run the best gambling house in town. There'll only be one. I'll shut down the other two. I want you to run the place on a fifty-percent share of the profits."

Poker Alice snorted and took a long pull on the cigar and blew two perfect smoke rings that worked their way slowly toward the ceiling.

"Fifty percent? We have house dealers at every table or charge players to buy chips?"

"Anyway you want to run it, just so the men like to gamble there."

"I'll think about it. Could I make a thousand dollars a week?"

"Not sure. There probably isn't that much money floating around in a town this size. But it would be secure and long term, as long as the gold vein holds out."

Poker Alice looked at him. She had a brief flash of a feeling that something wasn't quite right. Then she remembered. "Didn't I hear that the mine was played out, that it was about ready to close down? What's more, you don't own that saloon we were in."

Fairfax grinned. "So far that's just a rumor about the mine and the town closing down. If the mine does close for a week or so, the property values around here would be down to almost zero. A smart man could buy up the deeds for a penny on the dollar."

Poker Alice grinned. "You bluffing son of a bitch! You're as sneaky as I am sometimes. You plan on buying the mine from the present owner?"

Fairfax looked around, but they had been talking quietly and no one could hear them.

"You don't need to know that. If what should happen happens, the mine will be closed for two weeks, and then it will reopen with two shifts instead of just one. This little town will boom again. Gambling will be big business and we'll have a monopoly on the whole of it." Fairfax watched Alice and she showed him a small grin. "Well, Poker Alice, what do you think? Your name alone will bring a lot of gamblers into town just so they can say they played poker against the great Poker Alice."

"Flattery still works, doesn't it? Hell, let me sleep on it. Sure a possibility. I'm tired of traveling all the time. Might be good to sit down for a spell in my own house instead of a damn hotel all the time."

"Two days. I have to know in two days."

"Like hell you do. If you're closing down the mine for two weeks, I got two damn weeks to decide." She took a pull on the cigar and blew the smoke toward Fairfax. "Now get the hell out of here and let me think about the deal and smoke in peace."

At the office of the Gold Ledge Number One gold mine, Spur McCoy had waited two hours for Dooley Fairfax to return. A fuzzy-cheeked clerk in the mine office said Fairfax had gone down town and would be back in half an hour.

Two hours later Fairfax still wasn't there. Spur waited another hour until the miners left the tunnel; he was about to walk down the road to town when a man came marching into the office and sat down behind the big desk.

The clerk went over to the man and then came to see Spur.

"That's Mr. Fairfax. He says he can see you for two minutes. He still has to work out the final payroll for this week."

Spur had guessed the man was Fairfax and had inventoried him in a quick glance. He was about five feet ten, sandy-colored hair in a businessman's cut, a face more tanned than Spur figured would be right for a mining man. He wore town pants, a suit coat that didn't quite match, a white shirt, and a string tie. He had had no hat on when he'd come through the door.

As Spur walked up to the man he still wasn't sure how to play the meeting. He at last opted for a friend of the family. He saw that Fairfax had deep blue eyes. He was clean shaven with short sideburns and a small scar on his left cheek. His nose must have been broken as well since it took a slight jog to the left, making his handsome face that much more human and warm.

Spur held out his hand. "Mr. Fairfax, my name is Spur McCoy. I'm a friend of the Davis family. His widow is an old acquaintance and I'm here to help her take care of all the legal matters having to do with her husband's death. She asked me to find out all I could about it."

Fairfax touched his hand and waved at him. "Sit down, Mr. McCoy. The company will do all it can to help you. Davis was a good employee."

"I understand. What I can't understand is why Lester Davis was killed. Mrs. Davis and the other two Southern families in town said there had been almost no incidents of prejudice against them because they were from the South. As you can imagine, Mr. Davis's death came as a total surprise and shock to the three families."

Fairfax nodded. His eyes seemed riveted on Spur and alert to what he said. The man stood and walked to some bookcases and came back.

"This has troubled me and the rest of the town as well. No one seems to know just who these vigilantes are, how they operate, or who they will attack next. You may have seen the case of the tar and feathering today. Disgraceful. I'm trying to reach the town council to have a talk with them about some kind of tighter law enforcement. I don't want workers afraid to live here."

"One other thing, Mr. Fairfax. I was wondering if Lester Davis had been having any trouble with any of the men at work? Could some of the miners be the vigilantes?"

Fairfax looked thoughtful for a moment, combed his fingers back through his full head of sandy hair, and slowly shook his head. "I'd guess not, Mr. McCoy. I've worked with hundreds of these mining men. They don't go in for prejudices much. If a man can do the job, he's welcomed into that deep-mine fraternity. If he can't do the work, a crew will talk to the foreman and get him fired."

"So you don't think there could have been any connection between Lester Davis's job here at the mine and the fact that he was murdered?"

"Absolutely not. I'm sorry for Mrs. Davis, but I've done about all for her here that I can. Is there anything else?"

"No, I think that covers it. I'll have all the legal papers signed just as soon as I get back to the county seat. Thanks for your time and patience with my questions."

Fairfax and Spur got up. McCoy nodded at the mine general manager and walked out into the early evening.

By the time Spur made it back to town and found himself a spot in the hotel dining room, news that a miner had fallen to his death in a shaft late that afternoon had set the other diners to talking. Spur heard the news but it meant little to him. He hadn't heard the name of the man. He finished his dinner and was about to go up to his room when he remembered his promise to stay at Gwen Havelock's house that night. He turned toward the desk clerk just as Mrs. Davis hurried in the front door and looked around.

She saw him and walked over to him with a deliberate stride. Spur could smell trouble. He took the woman's arm and led her to the farthest corner of the lobby, where they sat down on a small couch.

"Mrs. Davis, you look as if something is wrong."

"There is. The other day when we talked, I was going to tell you who Lester worked with at the mine. I thought he might know something about the secret job they were on. Somehow you and I never talked about it. Then today I heard the news about the accident at the mine.

"The man who died was Fremont Ewing. He was a good friend of Lester's. He was the one who worked with Lester on that secret project. Isn't it strange that both of them have died?"

Spur scowled at her and nodded. "Extremely strange, Mrs. Davis, and I don't believe it was just a coincidence. I don't believe in chance. I have to find out exactly what kind of a job they were working on in the mine."

"I wanted to tell you that our two friends from Alabama also work in the mine. I talked to both of them tonight. They said they thought Lester worked with Fremont. Tomorrow they're going to see what they can learn at the mine about where Fremont died and what work he had been doing with Lester. They'll be careful not to attract any attention."

Spur nodded. "Good. They can get into the mine a lot easier than I can. Talk to them every night after their shift. If they find out anything, get in touch with me here at the hotel." Spur frowned a moment. "Have you noticed anyone hanging around your house at night? Has anyone been bothering you?"

Charlotte Davis shook her head. "Nothing out of the ordinary. My two neighbors are there for me. Our three families are extremely close."

"I think I better walk you home. It's dark out there. We don't want any more coincidences to take place. I don't want to worry you, but this is turning into a deadly affair in more ways than one."

They walked out the front of the hotel and down Main Street. Spur chose the side with only one saloon. After they got past it, he relaxed a little. He had spotted no one following them. But still, if it turned out that Lester Davis knew something important enough that he was killed because of it, the killers might suspect he had told his wife.

At the Davis home, McCoy stepped into the dark house and lit a lamp. When the lamp glowed, Charlotte lowered the shades in the front room and watched him a moment.

"Would you like to stay for a cup of coffee? I can get a fire going in just a minute."

"No, I think I should be heading back to town."

She frowned and looked away. "Mr. McCoy, I would feel a lot better if you could stay a few minutes. The house seems so lonesome now that Lester is gone."

"Have you thought of moving in with one of your friends here?"

"Yes, we've talked about it, but they both have families of their own. They don't need a widow lady taking up space."

Spur smiled at that. "Mrs. Davis, I'd be pleased to stay a few minutes and have coffee with you. I'll see to locking the back door and the windows. If they don't have locks on them, I'll nail them down. I'm not trying to frighten you, but being prepared is half of any battle."

He came back a few minutes later and found twist locks on the windows and a bar set for both front and back doors. The stove was hot and Charlotte put the coffee on to boil.

"Mrs. Davis, I think—"

She held up one hand. "Please, call me Charlotte. I was only married for about a year. Don't seem that long now. Lordy, how I miss that man."

Spur nodded. "Please call me Spur. What I was going to say is that your doors and windows are all secure, but I think it would be better for you if you spent the night at one of your neighbors."

Charlotte turned to look at him, her long blonde hair swirling around her shoulders. "You think that's best?"

"I really do. After we have our coffee, I'll go with you next door. We have to take care of you."

A tear seeped out of her eye and down her cheek. "I can't tell you—" She stopped and stepped close to him and rested her head on his shoulder. His arms went around her and she sighed softly, then looked up at him. "I don't know how I can ever repay your friendship."

Her face lowered against his chest and he could feel her breast pressing against his chest. His arms tightened around her.

"Just don't worry about that. We'll get to the bottom of this. Then you'll have to decide what to do. Will you go back to Alabama?"

"Oh, no." Her face came up again close to his. "I don't have any kin there. Some died in the war and my brother came west somewhere. I lost track. Just him and me now."

Spur knew he shouldn't but he lowered his face slowly toward hers. She saw him coming and at the last minute lifted her lips to touch his. It was a polite, gentle kiss and he pulled back but still held her.

"I know I shouldn't have done that," Spur said.

"No, it's all right. I could have stopped it. I liked it. No man has held me for almost a month and a half now. I get so lonely sometimes. Again?"

She reached up and he met her and this time the kiss was more demanding. She turned so both her breasts pushed hard against him and her leg pressed against his crotch. The kiss lasted longer and this time she was the one who pulled away.

"Yes, that is fine," she said so softly he barely heard her.

Spur let his arms come away from her but she continued to stay against him, her arms around him now. She looked up and he saw her face soft, beautiful in the faint light. She smiled and he watched her.

"Once more, Spur. Then I think I'll be able to get through the night in a strange bed. Please?"

He found her lips again and this time his hand gently caressed her breasts. Charlotte whimpered as he touched her and her tongue brushed his lips but he didn't open them. When his lips left hers her hand came up and held his hand over her right breast.

"Thank you, Spur. You've made me feel like a woman again, like I'm worth something. I know I can get through the night now. This was so delicious. Maybe sometime later—"

"Maybe, later. I think that coffee is done."

They sat close together on the sofa, sipping coffee and talking in low tones. She told him about her childhood in Alabama and how the war had ruined everything for her family. After the war she had met Lester when he returned from the fighting. They were married almost at once, then sold everything they had and came west.

When the coffee was gone, she took a few things in a satchel and he walked with her to the house next door. Betty Lou Clinton came to the door and hugged Charlotte.

"About time you got some sense, girl, and come live with us."She looked at Spur. "You want to come in for some coffee, Mr. McCoy?"

He thanked her and declined. Then he said good-bye and hurried away through the night. He had another engagement high on the hill overlooking the town. Tonight was a sleeping night, if he could convince Gwen of the plan.

Chapter Six

Nathan R. Havelock arrived in Gold Ledge on the morning stage from Colorado Springs. Havelock looked too common to be rich. He dressed like a struggling merchant in an old black suit with frayed cuffs, a white shirt, and a poorly adjusted tie. Wearing no hat, he stood on the boardwalk in front of the stage depot looking for someone to carry his one bag.

Havelock's squat body was more rotund than plump. His cheeks were full and his small blue eyes stared at the world as if they didn't yet quite comprehend that he was rich and powerful. He walked with a gentle swagger, not out of pride, but to prevent the movement from become a waddle. He was 60 pounds too heavy and didn't give a damn.

No one appeared to carry his bag, so he picked

it up and walked down the street toward his house. By the time he had moved half a block, a dozen men and women had crowded around him, all shouting questions.

"Are you closing down the mine?"

"Should we sell out our business and move?"

"Isn't there more gold up there you can find?"

"When will the mine be closing?"

"How can you close the mine and kill the whole town of Gold Ledge?"

Havelock held up both hands and the people fell quiet. He stared at the small crowd with surprise. He had learned how to handle people over the years, and he frequently put that knowledge to work.

"I have not announced that the mine is closing. Anyone who has is a liar. I'm here on my usual inspection tour. I'm in hope of pushing production and moving the mine into a two-shift operation, eight hours each shift. That will mean twice as many workers, twice as many foremen. Remember that."

"I'm on my way now to the mine to talk to Mr. Fairfax. I'm sure he'll have good news for all of you soon. Now, is there one of you who would take my bag up to my house? I have important business at the mine."

The crowd faded away until only one tall youth stood there watching Havelock.

"I'll do it for a quarter," the youth said.

Havelock nodded, tossed the boy a quarter, and struck out for the mine without looking back. The young man picked up the heavy portmanteau and lugged it down the street that led to the mine owner's house.

Havelock barged into the mine office and found

the clerk busy at his desk and the manager concentrating on a tablet of paper. Fairfax looked up and stood quickly.

"Mr. Havelock, welcome to the Gold Ledge. I wasn't expecting you."

"Figures," Havelock said and motioned his manager to sit down so he could have the dominant position. "Just where the hell are these rumors coming from about closing the mine?"

"I don't know how they got out, sir. I wrote you last week that we had no luck at all in those discovery tunnels we dug. The main vein looks as if it will produce ore for little more than a week. It's tapering off, sir. I've seen it happen before."

"Show me," Havelock said.

Twenty minutes later they were in the second level, which was not much more than 30 feet underground. They were at the end of the second-level tunnel, where heavy hammers pounded on twist drills as the men dug into the rocky formation to get ready to blast loose the white quartz rock in the vein that held the gold.

Halifax bellowed out a command and gradually the ringing of steel against steel stopped and the men looked and saw Havelock. They parted so he could examine the face of the tunnel.

Halifax pointed to the rock and motioned. "See the seam of the white quartz here that holds the gold ore. A month ago this quartz strata was two feet thick. Now it's less than a foot thick and it's growing smaller with each blast." He lowered his voice so only Havelock could hear. "It looks like damn sure that this vein is going to peter out within a week at most."

"How many discovery tunnels did you dig?"

"Six, the way you told me to. I put them in places where I figured there could be other seams and veins of gold. We went sixty feet with all of them and found nothing but rock and dirt."

"You're the mining engineer, Fairfax. Are there other areas that look favorable for searching tunnels?"

Fairfax motioned the mine owner back the way they had come. He nodded to the foreman at the tunnel face, then bellowed out an order and the men went back to work.

When Fairfax had the mine owner down the dimly lit tunnel far enough so they could talk in normal tones over the ring of the hammers on cold steel, he explained.

"We've given it the most logical try. There could be one or two other spots that might be productive, but six out of six is two strike outs in a row, and that's not good baseball."

"I know nothing of the game. Is it good mining logic you're using here?"

"About finding a new vein, yes, it's logical, Mr. Havelock. About keeping it from the men, I'm afraid they can tell that this vein is petering out as well as we can. They must have started talking. This is a one-business town. If the mine goes down, the town will vanish within a month."

"No hope at all?"

"I'll show you all of the discovery tunnels we dug. It cost a lot of money to drill and dig them out so I want to lead you down each one. There just isn't any indication at all that there is another vein near this one. If the vein was ruptured and carried say a mile away in some ancient disruption, there's no chance we could ever locate it."

Gold Ledge Gold Diggers

"Let's go look at those damn exploratory tunnels," Nathan Havelock said.

Fairfax nodded. "I think it's good that you see them. Then you'll know just how hopeless this hole in the ground is."

Three hours later, the two men sat alone in the mine office. Fairfax had sent the clerk on an errand. He turned in his desk chair and faced his employer.

"Well, Mr. Havelock, what do you think now about the life of Gold Ledge Number One?"

"I'd say your week's estimate looks about right. You said the production of quality ore is down to fifty percent of what it was when the vein was twice this large. That means it's going to drop another fifty percent right along until it ends in a mass of worthless rock."

"I'm afraid so, Mr. Havelock. I've worked a lot of mines. When the time comes to shut down, that's the only thing to do. No sense throwing two or three thousand dollars a day into a worthless hole."

Havelock stood, squared his shoulders, and walked slowly around the office. He came back and held out his hand. "All right, if that veins continues to peter out, you close the mine the day you run out of ore. This is your verbal authority to do that. Inform me by wire from Colorado Springs. I'll be in Denver. I might stay around here a couple of days to see how it goes."

"I think that's the only decision we can make under the circumstances." Fairfax stood and looked his boss in the eye. "One more thing I've learned about the mining business. When a mine is dry, the only thing left of any value is a salvage operation. Do you want me to stay on for a month or so salvaging the track and ore cars and lifts and cable that we can to sell on the market in Colorado Springs?"

"Is there a market?"

"A rather good one. Not a lot of money involved. I'd say with transportation costs and a broker's fee, you could clear maybe two thousand dollars to salvage the equipment from the mine here."

Havelock waved a hand. "Not worth the trouble."

"Then could I have the salvage rights? I'd need a contract and need to pay you ten dollars to make it legal."

Havelock waved again. "Whatever you'd like to do. Hell, I'll sell you the whole damn mine for ten dollars just as soon as that vein runs dry. I've made enough money off it. Let you make a few thousand for the equipment."

"That sounds good to me, Mr. Havelock. There's a lawyer you can use here in town. Should I see him tonight and have him draw up the papers?"

"Why not. Like you said, when the dance is over, it's time for everyone to walk his best girl home."

Fairfax turned to get pen and paper, and a big grin split his face. When he turned back to the mine owner, he was composed again.

"I'll make some notes for the lawyer," Fairfax said. " The contract will take effect the day that we judge that the vein has run out. I'll use three witnesses to the fact."

Havelock shook his head. "No, I need to revise that. I'll have the lawyer I use draw up the bill of sale and I'll stay until the vein runs out. I don't like to leave things tentative. I can find something to do in town for three or four days."

"There's usually a good poker game going down at the Deep Shaft Saloon," Fairfax said. "Last night the famous Poker Alice was playing."

"You don't say? I might just give the game a whirl, if I can find a good place to eat."

Spur got away from the house on the hill early that morning. He and Gwen had decided one round of tender lovemaking would be all they would allow themselves the night before, so Spur awoke rested and ready to do some tracking. He had decided his best lead still was the small real-estate man.

This time when McCoy strolled by the office the land seller was inside, so Spur sat across the street watching the place. Twice Odell Vail came out of his office, locked the door, put up a closed sign, and walked away.

Spur followed him. The first time he went into the general store and didn't come out. When Spur went inside, he found that the small businessman had left by the back door.

The second time Spur followed Vail from his office he went to the bank and back to his place of business. It was almost noon when Vail came out the door again. This time he went into the Deep Shaft Saloon and Spur followed him inside quickly.

Vail turned and pretended not to see Spur, then walked straight to the back door as if he were going to the outhouse. Spur hurried toward the rear door and went through it. He never saw what hit him. The first whack came on his right arm, numbing it down to his fingers. Another crack hit him on the left leg and he dropped to one knee with the pain. Then there were at least three men all over him, kneeing him, punching him, jerking his six-gun from the holster, and tossing it aside.

Spur got in two good blows but he couldn't stand up to the surprise attack by the three men armed with ax handles. He went to both knees. The ax handles slammed into him again and again. They hit his chest, his back, his sides, and his arms.

The only thing the men avoided was Spur's head. Vaguely he realized they weren't trying to kill him or he'd already be dead. He was about to fall flat on his face when he looked up and saw one of the blurred faces staring down at him. Spur didn't know who it was. Then the man's knee came up sharply under Spur's chin, slammed his head back, and drove the last shreds of consciousness from his brain.

When something cold and wet hit Spur's face, he tried to brush it away. The pain of moving his right arm brought a scream of agony. More spots of cold wetness hit him, then more. Spur blinked, trying to get his eyes to stay open. At last they did and he saw that it was dark. The wetness was a gentle rain that must have blown up during the afternoon.

He was flat on his back in the alley. How had he ended up there? Then he remembered. He'd been following the little real-estate man and blundered into a well-laid trap. He could almost see the ax handles slamming into his body.

Slowly he moved his right arm, which was painful but not broken. He flexed his fingers. The men hadn't broken his hands or his thumbs.

Gold Ledge Gold Diggers

He tried the same on his other arm, then each leg—nothing broken that he could find.

Spur tried to sit up, bellowed out a scream of protest, and sank back down. His chest! A stabbing, roaring pain exploded in his chest when he tried to sit up. He took a deep breath and groaned. The pain came again, only not so intense. Every breath gave him cause to gasp.

A broken rib, sure as hell. He eased over to his stomach in the garbage-strewn alley and slowly pushed up to his knees. Yes, better. He caught hold of a wooden packing crate and hoisted himself to his feet. The pain slammed into him but he held on tight to the box and weathered through it. His six-gun was gone.

Vaguely he remembered the men stripping it out of his holster and throwing it down. They had pitched it away from the bar door. He went down on his hands and knees and searched the area. After five minutes he found the weapon. He checked the chambers. All empty. Figured.

He crawled back to the packing box and used it to help him raise himself to his feet. The pain brought a screech of protest.

McCoy decided there was no way he was going back to the hotel. He wanted as few people to see him this way as possible. Gwen was too far up the hill. Even if he went to her shop she could never get him up to the mansion.

He knew where he was going then. All flat ground, not quite two blocks away. Spur began the long, slow trip. He made it to the end of the alley and fell only once. That trip took him ten minutes. He made sure he turned the right way on the cross street and held one hand across his hurt rib, gripping his shirt on the far side. The pressure seemed to make the hurt rib feel a little better.

It was more than a half hour later when Spur dragged himself up the one step leading to Mrs. Davis's front door. He sat on the rough boards, reached out, and knocked on the door. It was only then that he realized there was no light in the house.

He struggled to his feet and walked toward the Clintons' house. Lights shined from three windows there. He got up the step and sat down. He banged on the door twice before the last of his strength drained away and he slumped on the small porch unconscious again for the second time that day.

Spur awoke to the sound of soft singing. He lay in a bed in a small room that had wallpaper on the walls, ceiling, and door and a kerosene lamp on the dresser.

He heard the singing again. A woman's high voice, clear and precise, sang a hymn. When the song ended, Spur tried to sit up, but the pain in his chest brought a wail of pain. Hurried steps sounded and someone rushed into the room.

Charlotte Davis looked down at him with worry lines around her eyes. "Spur! Spur! Thank God, you woke up. I've been nigh into purgatory fretting about you. Where do you hurt the most?"

He lifted his right hand and touched his chest on the left side about halfway down.

"Rib," he said through swollen lips. "Broken, I think."

"Well, I can do as much for you as any old doctor. We'll just put some wraps around your chest to hold that rib tightly in place and then give you a hot toddy to ease the pain. Unless you want some whiskey. We have some around here some place."

Spur let her take the sheet down from his chest and he quickly saw that he was naked. "Who—"

Charlotte grinned, let her long blonde hair swing around to half cover her face, then brushed some dark hair back from his forehead.

"We found you on the step. Whit and Jeremy carried you over here to my place and stretched you out on the bed. Then I shooed them away and Betty Lou and I got you into bed and put some arnica on your cuts and bruises. Betty Lou had some white-vinegar tincture made from arrow-root, balm, and flowers she likes, so we used that, too. Lord, I didn't think you were ever going to wake up. It's been more than three hours now."

She took a big breath when she was through and stepped up beside him. "I hope you don't mind our undressing you."

"No modesty when a person is hurt bad."

Charlotte came over and pulled down the sheet to his waist and began to push with her fingers at various places on his chest and his stomach and down almost to his hips.

"Hurt anywhere? Does this hurt? What about this?"

She found no sore spots on his torso except his ribs. She leaned back and nodded. "Good, you must not be busted up anywhere inside. Had me real worried. At least you ain't spitting any blood."

She bent and kissed his cheek. "Now, I'll get some strips of an old sheet and we'll get your chest wrapped up to protect that rib. Might hurt a little, but it's what any sawbones would do and I can do it too."

It did hurt but Spur gritted it out. He saw that his hands and arms were clean. She must have washed him too. When the blonde lady came back in, he caught at one of her hands and she sat on the edge of the bed.

"Is this your bed?"

She nodded. "Been some time since I've had a good-looking man in my bed." She laughed making a joke of it, but he saw the hunger in her eyes.

"Thanks for all of this. You're more than repaying me for anything the government can do for you. Now, where are my pants?"

She shook her head and pushed down on both of his shoulders.

"Mr. Spur McCoy, you aren't going anywhere. Not tonight, not for at least two days. My pa was a doctor down in Alabama. Did I tell you that? I was about halfway to doctoring myself. It's been mostly what I heard for fifteen years."

"Two days?" Spur asked.

"Two days. I have you all to myself, unless Betty Lou comes over. Now you hush. I have some soup for you. I made fresh noodles tonight after you came to visit. I figure that will do you as much good as most of those ointments and doctoring pills."

Charlotte hurried to the door and Spur admired the way her skirt pulled tight across her little bottom. He smiled and then the mists came again and he drifted off to sleep.

When Spur awoke the next time, someone was gently rubbing his shoulders. He looked up, and saw the blonde hair, and called her name and she came in front of him.

Gold Ledge Gold Diggers

"Good. I woke you up. You need old Doc Charlotte's healing soup." She brought him a bowl with some hard crackers, toast, and jam. After he'd eaten it all, she smiled and told him to go back to sleep. She'd have some breakfast for him in the morning.

Spur wanted to ask where she would sleep, but somehow the effort overwhelmed him. He shut his eyes and tried to smile, but he slept before the start of a smile broke through.

The next day, Spur let Charlotte care for him like a battered puppy. When she brought him supper that night, he told her it was time for him to leave.

"I don't want you to go yet," Charlotte said. "At least not until morning. Nothing much you can do tonight." She rubbed the soreness in his neck and he felt himself relax. When he had finished eating, he let her take the tray away. Then she came back.

Charlotte knelt down beside the bed and watched him. "Spur McCoy, can I speak plain with you?"

"I hope you always do."

"The other day when you were here, I kissed you and you kissed me, and we got a little excited. Well, I don't know about you but I was really excited. I was wondering if you could kiss me again?"

Spur laughed softly and took her head in both hands and kissed her lips hard. He brushed his tongue against her lips, which parted at once. The kiss lasted a long time and he could sense her fires building. When he let her head go and her lips eased away from his, Charlotte sighed softly. Then she reached back and kissed his lips

87

a dozen times softly and with quick little moans of pleasure.

She leaned back from him then, smiling, and began to unbutton the fasteners on the top of her dress. She didn't say anything, just kept opening the buttons and smiling. Then she bent to kiss him again.

Chapter Seven

Spur watched the blouse open and reveal the marvelous view of Charlotte's bosom. Before he had hurt so much he hadn't even noticed her fine breasts stretching the white fabric of her blouse. As they opened out like a flower, he caught his breath. When both swung into view and Charlotte bent over him where he lay on the bed, he had the full effect of the large twin pendulums swinging in front of him with cherry-red nipples and soft pink areolas.

"Spur McCoy, please stay the rest of the night. I'd be ever so grateful if you would."

Charlotte straddled his legs with her knees and put her hands on each side of his shoulders so she hung in the air directly over him. Then she lowered one breast to his face. He kissed it, then licked her nipple, making her gasp and moan with delight. Slowly he pulled her orb into his mouth, chewing on the tender flesh gently and sucking on the nipple until she shuddered.

He moved his mouth to her other breast and gave it the same ministrations. As he did, his hands crept up her inner thighs, massaging the flesh, bringing shivers to her whole body.

"Oh, God, Spur, I can't stand it any longer." She moved and lay down beside him on the bed, careful not to touch his chest. Her hands went down the sheet and pulled it away from him. Then she touched his crotch and stared in amazement at the shaft that had grown there.

"My, oh, my!" she cried in wonder. "He was just a little guy before. Look at him now." Her hand closed around his erection and she slowly pumped him back and forth. She caught his hand with hers and pushed it between her open legs.

Spur brushed away her skirt and put his hand on the softness at her crotch, covering the cotton underthings and squeezing her heartland. A low moan came from Charlotte. Her legs spread wider and he found the top of her bloomers and pulled them down, thrusting his hand to her softness. Gently he traced her outer lips and she sighed, pushing her hips upward to keep the contact.

Then his finger slipped into the slot and drove it inward as far as it would go. The thrust brought a small cry of wonder and delight and she thrust her hips upward against his finger, pulled back, and pushed upward again.

"Yes, darling. Yes, yes. That feels wonderful." She stroked his erection faster until he stopped her. He pushed himself up to a sitting position and pulled his hand from her crotch and tugged at her dress. She sat up and took it off over her head, discarded a chemise, then kicked off her bloomers.

She sat there a minute beside him, as naked as he was. Then she kissed his chest around the tightly wrapped bandage and worked down to his upthrusting erection. She kissed the tip of him, then down the sides and back to the top. She looked at Spur, who nodded.

Slowly she let her lips slip around the purple arrowhead of his penis until it was fully in her mouth. Then she sucked on it and gently bobbed back and forth with her head. When Spur stopped her with a touch, she came away from him, lay down beside his naked body, and spread her legs.

"Please, Spur, right now. Do me now. I want you deep and hard inside me, so deep it hurts. Right now, Spur!"

He moved to his knees between her legs. Most of his hurts had faded. His chest still burned like fire when he moved too quickly, but other than that, he had mended. He knelt between her white thighs, then lowered himself. She lifted and he probed gently; then he slid into her.

"Oh, Lordy!" Charlotte whispered. "Oh, Lordy, but that is so fine. So fine. Darling, just so wonderful."

Her hips began to grind against his and he stroked a half-dozen times and waited, but she didn't climax. He tried again with the same result. Spur lifted up from her and slid his hand between them. He found her small node and twanged it once.

"What in the world?"

"You haven't touched this before?" he asked.

"Touched what? I don't know what you're talking about."

"Ask Betty Lou." He twanged the tiny node a dozen times and Charlotte erupted in a massive climax. She shivered and wailed and shook until he thought she would come to pieces. Then the spasms hit her five, six, seven times before she quieted down and opened her eyes to look at him.

"My God, but that was sensational. I don't think I've ever felt that way before. Not even the best times before were anything like that."

"That's a good thing to remember," Spur said. Then he could hold himself no longer. He lifted her legs, put them on his shoulders, and powered forward a dozen times, exploding like a pair of steam engines hitting head on. Steam hissed, parts of the engines shot into the sky and fell a quarter of a mile away, and Spur vaporized in the ecstasy of the moment. Then he came back to earth like a regular human being, saw the wavering face below him, and felt the daggering pains in his chest.

He had to roll away from Charlotte. He touched his bandages and she nodded. His arm went around her and she cuddled next to him, touching him with both hands.

"So marvelous," she whispered.

"It was wonderful."

They stayed that way for ten minutes; then Spur looked down at her. "Have the two men here found out anything about what Fremont Ewing and your husband were doing in the mine?"

"Not yet. They said there's a kind of blanket of secrecy over the two men. Nobody even wants to talk about them. Whit and Jeremy are still trying. Maybe tomorrow."

"Tomorrow I have to get back on the job. Enough of this lying around."

"But your rib is still broken."

"It will be for another six weeks. I can't wait that long. If nobody punches it, I'll be fine. I'll have it covered up with my shirt and jacket."

"I don't want to let you go, especially not after tonight. Are you strong enough to make love again?"

Spur grinned and chuckled. "I can't recall but one time when I wasn't strong enough. That's when I was almost dead. Sure, I'm strong enough for twice, maybe three more times."

Charlotte covered her face with one hand. "Oh, Lord! I've never done it more than once in a day since my wedding."

She broke her record that night.

The next morning, Spur felt almost normal. His rib hurt when he moved the wrong way, so he walked with his right thumb hooked in his pants belt. That took some of the strain off his chest.

He had to find out what Lester Davis and Fremont Ewing had worked on. From his talk with the mine manager, McCoy had gotten the impression that the man didn't like him and that he would tell Spur no more than was absolutely necessary. So that was out. The two miners from the South were having trouble getting any information inside the mine, so Spur figured his chances of talking to the miners themselves were less than zero.

What did that leave him? Spur had eaten breakfast at Charlotte Davis's house and walked uptown, trying to figure out what to do. Now he knew. The widow Ewing. Her man might have told her something about his secret job. Spur found out at the general store where the Ewing's lived and walked the three blocks to their small, well-tended house.

It had a fresh coat of white paint. There were lilacs, hollyhocks, and a rosebush growing beside the steps. McCoy knocked on the door and a moment later it came open. A tall, thin woman stared at him a moment, then nodded.

"Yes, I've seen you around town."

"I'm Spur McCoy, a friend of Charlotte Davis. I understand your husband worked with Mr. Davis. Could I talk to you for a few minutes? It might be better if I wasn't seen here at your front door any longer than necessary."

She closed her eyes a moment. "Yes. Yes, of course. Please come in. I'm Iona Ewing."

The clean house was sparsely furnished, but with all the taste the Ewings could probably afford. Iona waved him into the living room, and they sat on a sofa that had seen better times.

"Mrs. Ewing, I'm sorry about your husband. It's a tragedy and it probably wasn't an accident. I think both your husband and Lester Davis were killed for some reason. What that reason is is the part I haven't found out yet."

"It wasn't an accident?" Her face flared with anger and a touch of fear. "I don't understand. They told me he slipped when a ladder broke and fell down a shaft. I—"

"I'm not certain yet, Mrs. Ewing, but it's too much of a coincidence that your husband and Mr. Davis both died. I understand your husband worked with Mr. Davis on some secret project at the mine."

"Well, yes. Fremont did mention that he was working with Lester. There wasn't any secret about that."

"This secret job interests me, Mrs. Ewing. Did your husband ever tell you what it was about?"

She looked away. Her hands fumbled together in her lap, then went to her sides, only to return to her lap, and twist a handkerchief Spur hadn't seen before.

"What did he tell you, Mrs. Ewing? It could be terribly important."

She looked up. "He promised his boss he wouldn't tell anybody. Then he told me and made me promise not to say a word about it."

"Mrs. Ewing, I think that the project your husband worked on became so important that the mine people couldn't let him stay alive knowing about it. The vigilantes were a smoke screen to get rid of Davis, and the accident took care of the other man who knew something. The only way we can beat them is to find out what the project was and how the mine management is going to use that knowledge."

Spur reached into his pocket, took out a wallet, and extracted a thin metal card that he had glued to his new identification. It showed a tintype picture of him and stated that he was an agent of the United States Government Secret Service. It had his own signature and that of the President of the United States.

On the back side it said he had the rank of full colonel in the United States Army and would be accorded all privileges due his rank. He had the power to commandeer any federal or military forces, supplies, and equipment as he felt were needed.

Mrs. Ewing read both sides of the card and gave it back to him.

"It isn't just you against them, Mrs. Ewing. The United States Government is concerned. I was sent here because of the lynching of Lester Davis by the vigilantes. But this has taken on a new significance with your husband's death. Please, tell me anything your husband said about his job. It could be vital to the whole town."

Iona Ewing wiped tears from her eyes and nodded. "I'll tell you what I remember. It didn't seem important at the time. Fremont told me that he and Lester had been assigned to dig an experimental tunnel into a new section of the mine away from the regular workers. He didn't tell me what they were hunting or if they found anything, just that they had the job to run a small crew to dig into a new area underground."

"Did your husband change after he started digging the new tunnel? There must have been rumors about the mine closing for weeks. Did the two of you make any plans about moving to another town?"

"Yes, how did you know? I guess a lot of people in town were thinking the same way. Still are. But then after they had been on the job for two weeks, my Fremont stopped talking about moving. He said we might just settle down here for a few more years after all."

Spur looked up quickly. "He said you might settle down here?"

"That's what he said. Kept talking about how this could be a nice little town and we could raise our kids here."

"Did he say anything about the mine?"

"No, not that I remember."

Gold Ledge Gold Diggers

"But two weeks before you were talking about moving because the mine was about ready to run dry. There's only one reason he would want to stay here. The mine is not played out; there is still a lot of gold ore to be mined."

"But how could Fremont know that?"

"That's what I need to find out. I have an idea, but that will take some investigation on my part. You've been a big help, Mrs. Ewing. Now I have to get back to work."

McCoy thanked her again at the door, then hurried outside and down the block toward Gwen's Shop. Inside he found Gwen and her one seamstress. He and Gwen went into the back room to talk. Gwen kissed him firmly on his lips, put her arms around him, and hugged him soundly. Then she looked up.

"You have that expression on your face that says you can't wait to tell me something. What is it?"

Spur shook his head in wonder. Was he that obvious?

"Let me lay out a small story for you. One of the miners is talking with his wife about moving out of town since the mine is obviously playing out. No mine, no town. Then he has a special job at the mine, and two weeks later, the same man is talking about settling down in town and raising his kids here. He calls it a nice little town. What's your conclusion?"

"Easy. His special job at the mine has convinced him that the mine is not playing out, so he wants to stay."

"About what I've decided."

"What was the man's special job at the mine?"

"He and another man were assigned to run a small crew digging an experimental tunnel, evidently to try to find the old vein or a new vein of gold ore."

"And they found it. Why the secret? Why the mystery?" Gwen lifted her brows and her pretty face fell into a frown. "So somebody could buy a worthless mine that is not worthless at all. Buy it for a song or even a dollar to make the deal legal. I guess that's why Daddy's in town—someone is trying to steal the mine from him."

"Precisely. Do you know if he's thinking of closing down the mine and selling it?"

"Daddy never did like the mining business. He's rich enough now to sell it for a dollar and live high on the social calendar in Denver for the rest of his life."

"But he wouldn't want to get swindled. You have to tell him under no circumstances to make any deal to sell the mine without letting me talk to him?"

Gwen nodded. They went into the front of the store and she sat at a small desk and wrote two notes. She sealed both, then wrote her father's name on them.

"I'll send one to the mine and one to the mansion. He should get one of them. I want you to come to dinner tonight at seven. We're having a special feast because Daddy came."

"Miss Havelock, I'll be there. If you see your father before I do, warn him what I think is happening."

Spur waved at the woman and went back to the street. He felt better already. If he was right, he might have the whole scheme figured out. But he had no idea who the villian in the piece was.

Gold Ledge Gold Diggers

Maybe one of the tunnel bosses or a foreman or even the general manager. It could be anyone who could cover up the results of one of the exploratory tunnels.

That same man would have to be one of the vigilantes or have the ear of one of them. That way he could get Lester Davis hung on the pretense that he simply was a hated Rebel from Alabama.

How would the plotters keep the news of the new vein from the rest of the miners? It would have taken eight or ten men to make much progress on a tunnel. When the first indicators had come, most or all of the men would have been sent away, and the two lead men could have picked and shoveled out the last few feet and found the vein. They would then have reported the good news to their secret bosses.

That would have explained the rumors about the mine being shut down. Such rumors would grow and people would start leaving town and the owner would see the move and believe that the vein was running out. So he'd sell the mine cheap and go back to Denver and be a rich old man and chase the young girls who wanted his money—or so went the theory McCoy was determined to prove.

Spur arrived at the mansion where the Havelocks lived at a quarter to seven. Nathan R. Havelock sat in his study, looking out over the city and smoking a big cigar. He turned when Spur came in.

"McCoy, isn't it? My daughter told me you had some crazy idea about somebody trying to swindle me out of the mine."

"Indeed, Mr. Havelock, I do." Spur told the millionaire his suspicions and the small man snorted.

"Lots of charges, but where's the proof, McCoy? Tell me how you can prove this."

"I can't prove it yet, but there are some circumstances I think will interest you. Two miners who were lead men on the crew that dug one of the experimental tunnels are both dead. One was hanged by the local vigilantes for being a Southern Rebel. The other man died yesterday in a fall in your mine. Isn't that a coincidence that both men who might know about a new vein of gold in your mine suddenly died violently?"

"Interesting, but not proof."

Spur told Havelock about Fremont Ewing and how he had changed his mind about leaving the town after he worked on the experimental tunnel.

"Ewing had to know that there was gold in the mine or he would still want to leave town. Half the men out there right now are making plans to leave the second the mine closes."

"Now that is more convincing. Why would somebody try to cover up the experimental tunnel results?" Havelock stopped a minute and nodded. "Yeah, easy. So he could prove the mine was running out of gold ore. So he could buy it for ten dollars. Then a day, a week, or a month later he could reopen the mine and get rich himself."

Havelock stood and paced his study, puffing smoke from his cigar like a steam engine struggling up a sharp grade with a long string of cars behind it.

"By damn! The audacity of that mongrel. I trusted him and gave him a chance. Some men

I know in Denver told me not to trust him. They claimed to have proof that he'd done some sneaky things just short of criminal. I trusted the rattlesnake."

"Who is it, Mr. Havelock? I work for the federal government. I can arrest him tonight and charge him with conspiracy to commit grand theft. He'll go to prison for ten years."

"No. This is a man I trusted and I want to take care of him myself. If there's anything left of him, I'll bring him around for you to arrest. I deserve my time with him first."

Havelock took a legal form from his jacket pocket, lit it with a match, and dropped it in the fireplace. He watched it burn.

"We were supposed to sign the contract tonight. That son of a bitch! I'm going to have him sign something all right. He made a move with his right hand and a deadly little derringer lay in his palm. It was an over-and-under large caliber. "I'll settle with him once and for all."

"I'll be glad to come along," Spur said.

Havelock turned and growled. "Don't you dare. I've got two rounds here. Only need one for him. If you follow me, I'll use the other one on you. That damn clear, son?"

Spur nodded and Havelock stormed out of the house.

Gwen came in, her face splattered with a question.

"I told him about the swindle. He's going somewhere now to settle with the scoundrel. I tried to go with him, but he threatened me if I tried. It's something he has to do by himself."

They ate the dinner, which was deliciously done: pheasant, rainbow trout, spare ribs, several vegetables, and three kinds of pie for desert.

An hour went by and the mine owner hadn't come back.

"Where would he go?" Spur asked.

"Might be anywhere, but I'd bet the mine office. Anyone who could pull off a swindle like this would have to be at the mine to do it."

They both stood up at the same time and a minute later both ran from the house and up the road toward the mine and the small office.

They heard two shots and rushed forward. "Is there a back door?" Spur called. Gwen nodded. By then they were at the front door of the office. Spur drew his Smith & Wesson American and edged open the door. He heard nothing. He waited a moment and listened again.

"Help me," a faint voice said inside.

Spur went through the door at an angle and dived to the floor, his weapon up and covering the 20-foot room. He saw no one. The voice came again, more faintly. Spur leaped to his feet. A leg protruded from beyond a desk. He rushed over there and knelt.

Nathan R. Havelock lay on his back, his hand over his chest, where blood seeped through his fingers. Spur turned to see Gwen only a few steps behind him.

"Hurry. Rush to town and bring back the doctor. Your father's been shot and the wound looks serious."

Chapter Eight

Nathan R. Havelock was unconscious when Spur found him and still that way when Doc Gaylord arrived about fifteen minutes later. The doctor saw that the bleeding had stopped. He took another look at the hole in Havelock's chest and scowled.

"This is an exit wound, McCoy. This man was shot in the back."

"Figured that out, Doc. What I want him to tell me is who pulled the trigger. Then I'll go put the backshooter down and hang him. When will Havelock be able to talk?"

The middle-aged doctor shook his head. "I've seen men shot this way expire in seconds. Some I've seen live for days. One man talked a blue sidewinder for three days, got off his bed, and went back to work.

"Depends what the slug hit on its way through

the body. I'd say this one nipped a lung for damn sure. Not much more we can do for him right now. You want him taken to the mansion, Miss Havelock?"

"Yes, Doc. I'll have the night watchman hitch up a flat-bottomed wagon. We can take him down that way."

"Watchman?" Spur asked. Gwen nodded and he ran out into the mine yard and bellowed, "Night watchman, get out here. We need you."

Spur waited and called the message out again at the top of his parade ground voice. A man came from a small shack near the mine entrance. He obviously had been sleeping. He yawned, stretched, and snapped one suspender on his pants, shivering when the elastic hit his body.

"Yeah, you called me?"

"How long you been sleeping?"

"Don't rightly know."

"You hear any shots a few minutes ago?"

"Shots?"

Spur saw he was getting no where. "Find a flat-bottomed wagon and hitch up a horse to it. We have to take Mr. Havelock down to the mansion. Move now or your job here is over in ten minutes."

The night watchman shuffled off. Spur drew his six-gun and put a round six inches from the watchman's left foot. The man yelped and rushed forward to get the wagon ready.

At the mansion, Spur and the doctor eased Havelock onto his bed. Spur made sure Gwen would stay with her father and ask him who had shot him if he woke up and could talk. Then Spur left on a run.

He had to get into the mine and find that

tunnel to check for himself if it was a new strike. The Southern men might be his answer. He found all the Alabama natives at the Clintons' house. They had popped corn and made candy apples for one of the children's birthdays. Spur took the two men outside and explained his problem.

"So if either of you know where that experimental tunnel is, tell me. I need to get down there tonight and see what they found."

Clinton shuffled his feet and looked away. Then he swore under his breath and turned. "Hell, I know where it is. Found out today. My lead man said he'd have my ass fired if I ever went in there. He said he had it right from the top boss that it wasn't to be even thought about, let alone examined."

"Hell, I'll go too," Jeremy Towers said. "I never have liked that damn lead man. I'll get some of them sulfur matches and we'll go down and find a few torches. We can get past the night watchman easy. He usually sleeps all night."

A half hour later, the three men slipped past the sleeping night watchman and into the mine. They picked up kerosene-soaked torches, gave them another slosh of coal oil, lit one, and ran down the main tunnel. It went only 50 yards to the first shaft, which went down 15 feet to the second-level tunnel.

The vein of gold ore had slanted from the upper level down to the lower one. Then it went down only gradually, so the second tunnel wasn't on the level.

The three men went down the ladder to the second level; then they hurried ahead with the one torch lighting the way. They passed four branch holes dug back into the rock wall. Clinton shook his head.

"It's on down here and goes the other direction."

Another 20 yards ahead Clinton pointed and they turned to the right into a tunnel barely five feet high. They had to bend over as they worked ahead. The hole had been bored into the rock of the mountain for 50 feet. At the end they found where it was plugged by a pile of loose dirt and rocks.

"Damn," Clinton said. "This isn't a natural fall. Somebody blasted the end of this tunnel closed."

"Hiding the evidence," Spur said. "Anybody got a shovel?" They found three nearby, where more tools had been left. All three men began to dig to break through the plug.

After two hours of digging and resting and digging again their shovels hit solid rock.

"Damn again," Clinton said. They blasted it right next to the end. Probably used plenty of powder."

The men dug again. They ignored the dirt and rocks at their feet. All they wanted to do was dig away enough of the shrouding dirt to find any evidence of a vein of gold on the tunnel face.

Ten minutes later, Clinton pointed to the solid face of the tunnel. "White quartz. That's a damn good sign."

Another ten minutes and they had clawed down enough of the remaining rocks and dirt to reveal what they hoped to find. It was a large strata of white quartz over three feet wide. All through it they could see the glint of veins and clusters of gold.

"No wonder Lester was hanged," Towers said. "Somebody used that Southern stuff as an excuse to silence him."

"The other man too. Somebody wants everyone to think that the Gold Ledge Number One is a worked-out, worthless mine. Now we have to find out who."

Spur started to shovel dirt and rocks back over the exposed fortune in gold. The other two men looked at him a minute, then nodded. They had to cover it up so nobody else would know about it until the right time.

It was almost two o'clock in the morning when they came out of the mine. They hurried down to the town. Spur thanked the men and told them to keep the secret for another few days. At least they knew the mine wasn't closing, so they didn't have to make any plans to sell out and move.

Spur cut around to the other street and watched the Ewing house a few minutes. Then he went up to the rear bedroom, where he saw a dim light and rapped on the window. He did it three times and at last the light came up brighter and the lamp moved toward the window. The curtain swept back and tall, thin Iona Ewing held the lamp so the light showed out the opening. Spur pointed to the door in back and she nodded and headed that way. Spur waited on the porch as she unbolted the door. He stepped inside and she hugged her nightdress to her body.

"Mr. McCoy, is there some problem?"

He nodded. "Have you noticed anyone around? Has any one been bothering you?"

She shook her head. "Why should anyone?"

"Because your husband told you why you didn't have to worry about moving. He told you they had found a new vein of gold three feet wide in that experimental tunnel. I just saw it myself. If I could figure out your husband told you, so can the man who killed your husband. I think you better go to the hotel to spend the night. This could all be over tomorrow."

"I don't want to go anywhere. I have Fremont's six-gun."

"Have you ever fired it, Mrs. Ewing?"

"Well, no, but I can if I need to."

Before Spur could answer, a flaming torch crashed through the kitchen window. Spur caught up a bucket of water from the sink and threw it on the torch, putting the fire out. They heard another window crash in front and smelled the smoke.

"They must have seen me come inside," Spur said. Iona stared for the back door but Spur shook his head. "They'd be waiting for us there. Let me entertain them a little." He made her sit on the floor next to the inside wall, then he ran to the front of the house and looked out the window. He saw three men on horses, they were wearing white hoods and waving torches.

Spur broke out the small window in the front door and fired three times with his Smith & Wesson. He saw one man cringe and lean away. One horse bleated in pain, stumbled, and fell. Spur crawled away from the door, and a moment later, a dozen rounds blasted through it. He ran to the back of the house and checked both bedroom windows. He saw no one on the far side of the house away from the street.

"Over here, Iona. Out the window. Hurry. They'll be around here soon."

Spur lifted the bedroom window, knocked out a screen, and pushed his legs out. He jumped to the ground and reached up for the woman who was still in her nightgown. She put her legs out and then half fell into his arms. One of his hands caught her breast but he held on so she wouldn't fall. Then he carried her in his arms and ran into the darkness.

Spur and Iona could see the fire blazing on the front of the house. A few minutes later the fire broke through the roof. Spur left the woman hidden in some trees and circled the house. Two of the vigilantes still sat in front of the house on their horses. One fired into the burning building again.

Spur slipped up within 20 yards of them and then yelled, "Drop your guns or die where you sit."

One man whirled and fired. Spur tracked him a moment and fired. The slug caught the hooded man in the side of the head and jolted him out of the saddle. The vigilante was dead before he touched the ground.

Another vigilante brought his mount around but Spur's second and third rounds hit the roan in the neck. She went down in a spray of dust and the man hit the ground hard and sprawled in a curious tangle of arms and legs. A second later he brayed in pain. Spur put another round near him and walked up slowly.

"Hold both your hands in the air as high as you can reach or you're dead buzzard bait."

The man screamed in pain, but lifted his hands. Spur ripped the flour sack off his head and stared at the man's face in the pale moonlight. He was Quint Upton, the man who owned the general store.

Spur looked at him again. "Upton, why are you bellowing?"

"Broke my right leg. Run and get Doc Gaylord quick."

Spur chuckled. "Not a chance. You just tried to kill me and Iona Ewing, and now you want me to do you a favor? Hell, I should put a bullet right between your murdering eyes."

Upton's eyes widened and he began to shake. "No, no. Don't do that. I really didn't want to do this vigilante stuff. They made me come."

"Sure, Upton. Now let's see who the other vigilante over here is who right now is sitting on a hot bed of hickory coals in the devil's furnace room."

Spur pulled the flour-sack hood off the man, but didn't recognize him. "Who is your dead friend here, Upton?"

"Dead?"

"Like the ever present dormouse. Who is he?"

"Yale. Runs the livery."

"Well, ain't that convenient. I'd like to chat, but I've got a lady waiting for me. I'll just put these hoods back on your heads so folks can identify you easier in the morning. The doctor will get here in the morning. But I'll doubt that he'll want to set a broken leg just so you can hang. In the meantime, I'll tie your hands together behind you so you don't try to hobble anywhere. Might as well tie your ankles together too."

McCoy moved Upton's right leg so he could tie his ankles, and Upton gave a bleating scream when the broken leg was moved. Spur finished tying the legs, then punched Upton in the shoulder.

"Don't go anywhere. I'll be back in an hour or

so. Might want to put some brands on your face with some of the hot coals from the fire you guys started. That'd be fitting, don't you think?"

Spur walked around the blazing house. Two men stood down the way watching it burn. Spur called them and they came up. He pointed to the two hooded men.

"Couple of the vigilantes. Would you keep an eye on them until I get back. Don't want their buddies to come back and rescue them. Especially Upton there. We want him to tell us all he knows about the other vigilantes before he hangs."

Spur went back to where he had left Iona, told her what happened, then helped her walk two more blocks along the streets until they came to the Clintons' house. No lamplight showed. When Spur knocked on the back door, it opened an inch and a shotgun's twin muzzle poked through.

"State your business or get blasted," a rough voice called.

"Spur McCoy. I've got one more favor I need you to do."

With Iona safely tucked in at the Clintons', Spur went back to the burning hulk of Iona's house and sat down beside Upton. He poked the man's broken leg bringing a wail of pain.

"Upton, good man, glad you're awake. Now tell me, who are the other three members of your little murdering conspiracy?"

"Who are they? Hell, I ain't telling you. Why the hell should I?"

Spur hit the man's broken leg with his fist and Upton screamed in pain. "That's one good reason you have to tell me. It's one hell of a long time until morning. Looks like it's just you and me and that broken leg of yours. I wonder if it would hurt more if the bone tore through your flesh and found the open air?"

Upton stared at Spur through his tears and sucked in a long breath. "Damn you to hell, whoever you are. Too damn bad your mother didn't have any bastards who lived."

Spur slammed his fist into the broken leg again and this time Upton passed out.

It was five minutes before the merchant groaned and then bellowed in pain and came back to the land of the conscious.

"Damn you!" Upton snarled.

"We'll make it easy for you, Upton. That little real-estate man, Odell Vail—is he one of the gutless wonders calling himself a vigilante?"

"Why do you think he might be one of us?"

Spur told him about the Bateman brothers trying to roust him and how Vail suckered him into the alley where he was beat up.

Upton gave a short laugh, followed by a groan. "At least we got some revenge on you. Hell, yes, Vail is one of us. Not the brightest. You'll never find the other two. I won't say another damn word. You beat on me all you want."

Spur decided he'd probably milked all he could from the merchant. "All right, Upton, no more questioning. Get on your feet. I'm taking you down to the deputy sheriff's office and his one-cell lockup."

"I can't walk. My leg's broken."

"Tough shit, Upton. Hop on one foot for all I care. You tried to kill me, remember? I should leave you here as a second corpse. You want that? I can give it to you?"

Spur drew his Smith & Wesson and cocked

the hammer. Upton scrambled around, trying to stand. He found a branch from a tree and, using it as a crutch, got to his feet. Twice he screamed in pain as his weight came down on his right leg.

"Let's go," Spur said and walked toward the local law's office. Upton hobbled along behind, hopping and swinging his broken leg forward. Every few feet he'd cry out in pain as his leg hit the ground.

The walk to the deputy sheriff's place was slow. The lawman slept in back and Spur pounded on the door until he came in jeans and no shirt, with a shotgun in his hands.

"Got a prisoner for you. One of the vigilantes. Another one is dead near the Ewing house, two blocks over. This one and some others burned the place down and tried to kill the widow Ewing. I want this one charged with attempted murder, arson, the lynching of Lester Davis, and assault and battery on that gambler they tarred and feathered."

Spur had not met the deputy sheriff before. He was a wild-haired young man, lean and trim. He eyed Spur curiously.

"Heard you was in town. You a lawman of some kind."

"Yes. I'm Spur McCoy. I work for the United States Secret Service. I have jurisdiction here, I guarantee. You have a cell?"

"Yeah, one, right back here. I heard about you. Oh, I'm Deputy Sheriff Abner Lombard."

When they put Upton in the cell and locked the door, the prisoner said, "Abner, I got a broken leg. You got to call Doc Gaylord right away."

Spur shook his head. "Wouldn't bother the Doc

tonight. Let him get his rest. Upton's leg won't get worse by morning. You can bring the sawbones over then if you want to."

Abner frowned. "Upton here is one of the vigilantes?"

"True enough. The other one dead out by the burned up house is Yale, the livery stables man."

Abner shook his head. "Be damned. Never would have thought either one of them would be involved in this."

"There are still three more of them out there somewhere. What time is it?"

"After four in the morning. Less than an hour to sunup."

"Think I better go back up to the Havelock mansion. The mine owner got shot tonight by someone at the mine. Last time I saw him he was unconscious and couldn't tell us who did it. Doc said he couldn't tell how bad the chest wound was. Whoever shot Havelock hit him in the back."

"Be damned!" Abner looked as if all the crime in the country had suddenly swept in on him here in quiet Gold Ledge. "Who would shoot that old man?"

"That's what I aim to find out."

Spur left the deputy sheriff's small office and walked up the hill. He was feeling some stabs of pain from his chest. He slowed a little and his legs started telling him they'd had about enough exercise for one day.

He saw lights on in the mansion. He started to knock at the front door but it opened and Gwen stood there in the same dress she had worn for the dinner.

"He hasn't woken up yet, Spur. I'm frightened. Doc agreed to stay. He's napping in the room right beside Daddy's room. He just can't die, he can't. I wouldn't know what to do with the mine and his other interests."

"If he hasn't died yet, I'd say his chances must be good. The second he wakes up, we've got to get him to tell us who shot him and who is trying to steal the mine from him."

Gwen and Spur sat in chairs in the big master bedroom, watching the labored breathing of the mine owner. Spur told Gwen what had happened down at the Ewings' house.

"If you hadn't been there they would have killed her for sure," Gwen said. "You shot and killed one of them, you said. Who?"

Spur told her the names of the two vigilantes.

"Mr. Upton? He's been one of my good friends. He helped me get started in my shop. I'd never have guessed him. Mr. Yale is no surprise. He's always been on the slippery side. I think most of the horses he rents are stolen. Nobody could ever prove anything, but a lot of people suspected him. Now it won't matter much one way or the other."

They stared at each other. Nathan R. Havelock muttered something in his sleep and they rushed to his bed, but he only grumbled some words they couldn't understand and lapsed back into his sleep.

"Let's hope the unconsciousness will turn into normal sleep," Spur said. "I've seen that happen before."

Gwen said she hoped so. She moved her chair over next to Spur's and laid her head on his shoulder. His arm came around her and she slept.

Spur couldn't sleep. He had to be ready if the mine owner had anything to say. What McCoy wanted most was the name of the man who had tried to steal the mine from its owner. The same man must be one of the vigilantes. He would only get a prison sentence for trying to steal the mine. But for the vigilante lynching and the death of the other miner, he would hang. That was what Spur hoped for. All he had to do was find out who the man was.

"Come on, Nathan R. Havelock. Open your eyes and tell me who shot you," Spur said softly. But the mine owner was still unconscious.

Chapter Nine

The small Chinese girl brought Gwen and Spur coffee and muffins about six the next morning. Gwen awoke in the chair where she had slept the last two hours and tried to stretch out a crick in her back. She looked at Spur, who stood beside the bed.

Spur shook his head. "Still no reaction from him. He isn't just sleeping; it's deeper than that. He's still unconscious for some reason. Maybe the doctor will know some way to bring him out of it."

Gwen went in and woke the doctor, and he came into the bedroom. While looking at the motionless man, he frowned.

"I don't like it. He should be making some kind of a response by now. Let me try some smelling salts. Sometimes that's enough of a shock to get a man back into action."

117

The doctor waved the small bottle in front of the mine owner's nose several times, and on the last time Havelock snorted and coughed and his eyes came open.

"Trying to kill me? Who did that?"

But by the time Gwen had hurried to the bed, her father had settled back on the pillow and his breathing had taken on the same rapid, shallow rhythm it had had before.

Dr. Gaylord shook his head. "We'll just have to wait and see. We'll try the same thing about noon. The bleeding has stopped. He seems to be breathing adequately. There's nothing else we can do for him right now."

Gwen insisted that the doctor and Spur go down for breakfast. She'd eat later. Spur piled up the hotcakes and bacon and syrup and rich butter and began. He followed that with three eggs over easy, a cup of coffee, a slice of toast and strawberry preserves.

The doctor finished eating quickly and went back upstairs. He told Spur that he would stay there as long as there was any hope that his patient would regain consciousness.

When Gwen came down, she looked tired and drawn. Spur kissed her forehead and held a chair for her.

"He's going to make it. I know he will," Spur said. "The shooting was a shock to his system. He might have had a mental shock as well when he saw who had shot him. He'll weather all of this and be as good as new. You keep watch and ask who shot him when he wakes up. I've got one more lead to follow up to see if I can nail down the rest of the vigilantes."

Gold Ledge Gold Diggers

Spur knew it was past time to go after Vail, the real-estate man. Spur hoped the man hadn't run. If Vail had heard about the two vigilantes taken already, he might have taken off. Or did he have too much invested in Gold Ledge to run? How could a real-estate man be tied in with the swindle to take over a supposedly worthless mine?

Spur considered the situation as he walked toward the town. He passed the stamping mill that pounded the quartz ore into powder so the gold could be separated from the rock and quartz. The stamping mill was made up of six stampers, which sat side by side on heavy concrete foundations. Upright wooden columns a foot thick and three feet wide with a metal crossbar between them formed the frame for the stamper.

A heavy steel shaft went through the middle of the ten-foot-high structure. The shaft held eccentrics that lifted two-inch-thick steel rods. When the eccentric came to the flat part, it stopped lifting the steel rod and released it, letting it jolt downward and hammer the gold ore in the box below that held the ore.

There were five eccentrics on the steel shaft. All were set at different angles so the five hammers came down one at a time to strike the gold ore with tremendous force in the steel box, which was about two feet wide.

The shaft that turned the eccentrics was attached to a four-foot-thick flywheel, which was turned by a long belt around another pulley attached to a powerful steam engine on the ground at the end of the line of stamping mills.

The steam power kept the belt turning and the hammers pounding the gold ore into powder, which was then sifted down a shaking screen, and the pure gold filtered out from the lighter rock and quartz dust.

Spur had seen these mills before. He was surprised that this one had six sets of the five hammer units working. All were attached to the same power shaft, which came off the steam engine. He took one more quick look at them. They all were working as he walked on down the hill toward the outskirts of the town, less than 300 yards away.

He found the real-estate office open and turned the doorknob. He got inside just as a black-suited figure rushed through the back door.

Spur hurried to the door, threw it open, but remained against the wall beside the open door. A shot pounded through the empty space where the door had been; then another door beyond slammed.

Spur moved cautiously through the next room, edged the door open and looked out. He saw the same black suit vanishing inside a two-story building that he hadn't paid much attention to before.

He had no idea what kind of a store fronted it on Main Street. Back here it looked deserted, abandoned. It was four stores down. Spur ran to the door and realized that he didn't even feel a twinge from his cracked rib. Adrenaline shooting into his bloodstream must have overridden the pain, he decided.

At the back door, he pushed inward, heard a shot from inside, and saw the door rattle as it absorbed the bullet. He kicked the door inward and ran in low finding himself in a dark, musty warehouse.

He stopped and listened. He could see little. There were two windows high up toward the front of the structure. He guessed it was at least 70 or 80 feet long, half that wide. He could make out a partition here and there and a stairway along the far side. He heard a board squeak and stared that way. Somebody had moved on the stairs.

"You can run, Vail, but I'll get you eventually. Why not just give it up now and take your chances with a jury?"

His voice drew a shot from the stairs. Good, the little man had used up three rounds. He must have only two left. Spur was ready when Vail shot, and he fired a round just below the flash of the other gun. The round coming at Spur missed by six feet but he heard a wail of pain from Vail on the stairs.

"You might as well give it up, Vail. I know about the new strike at the mine. Your scheme won't work. You have no chance at all to swindle the mine from Havelock."

Spur still had plenty of shots left. The other man must have only one. Spur's voice had covered the movement of the small man, and by the time he had finished speaking, Spur figured the real-estate man had made it to the second floor. The section of the warehouse with a second floor covered about half the length of the building. The rest had the high roof overhead.

Spur's eyes had adjusted to the dim light. He ran for the stairs hoping to draw another shot, but the small man must have realized he had only one round left and no way to reload. Spur was banking on the idea that Vail had a percussion revolver, which would take lots of light and several minutes to reload the five rounds.

Spur went up the steps three at a time, but paused after he had ascended a dozen of the treads. He squatted and listened. He heard something above, but couldn't figure out what it was. He was just ready to take another surge up the steps when he saw something looming over him.

Almost too late he realized what it was. Enough light came in the second-story window for him to see that the object was a 50-gallon wooden barrel that lay on its side at the top of the steps. A second later the barrel rolled down the steps. It was as wide as the open stairs. Spur could see nothing to grip to try to pull himself up and over the path of the heavy barrel. He had no way to escape. Instinctively he knew what to do and did it instantly.

Spur went flat on the steps, lay tightly against the riser and hung his head over the far edge of the tread into the void. Just as he completed his flattening process the barrel thundered down the steps over him.

He lay on his stomach and felt the side of the barrel brush his buttocks as it raced by bouncing off the stair treads and careening down the stairs to smash into a wall at the bottom.

Once the barrel had passed him, Spur sprang up, raced forward, and fired one shot at the top of the stairs. He still had three rounds.

"Oh, damn!" the man up there wailed.

Then Spur was at the top of the steps, where he flattened against the wall and held his six-gun ready for a killing shot. Nothing happened.

Spur waited for the other man to move. Vail must be waiting too, perhaps trying to figure out what to do. Spur figured he could outwait the little real-estate man. If Vail was part of the scheme to swindle Havelock out of the mine, how else could he profit? It baffled Spur. Why would someone else need Vail? Could Vail have planned the swindle by himself? No, somebody inside the mine was needed to make the swindle work.

Spur heard a board creak maybe 30 feet across the dark second floor. Spur waited again. He had his Smith & Wesson cocked and ready to fire. Again there was a long silent time. Two, maybe three minutes, Spur estimated.

The next thing Spur heard confused him. It sounded like the upward slide of a double-hung window frame. He tried to remember. Was there a wall on the edge of the second-floor section? There must have been, and beams in the middle of the wide space to hold up the second-floor structure.

With A window, the man could jump from the second floor down to the first. Maybe go down on a rope, hold by his hands and drop not more than 12 feet. Spur raced halfway down the stairs. He could see the front of the second-floor section. Yes, walls and windows. The far one near the other side of the building had an open window.

Something came through the opening and fell. It sounded as if it could be a rope. A man came through the window in a rush, holding onto the rope in the darkness. Spur could see only bits and pieces and not enough to fire at. It was a double rope latch up with his foot in a loop at the bottom and Vail let his weight lower him quickly from the second story to the floor.

Spur had sprinted down the stairs, but the real-estate man darted through a side door letting a shaft of bright sunlight into the warehouse. For a moment the light blinded Spur; then his eyes adjusted and he ran for the open side door.

Outside he found he was beside the building that extended to the alley. Vail turned and looked over his shoulder at Spur as he raced around the end of the structure and up the alley toward the street.

Spur reloaded as he ran, pushing out the empty rounds and putting new rounds in the cylinder so he had six live rounds. At the street Vail turned uphill and headed for the stamping mill.

Spur held his reloaded six-gun in his right hand and began to sprint uphill. He brayed with a sudden sharp pain across his chest and slowed to a walk. He had twisted just wrong and the pain kept pounding through his chest.

He tried holding both his arms up. Then he crossed them. Finally he pushed them high over his head but the pain still came.

For a moment he stopped dead still. The pain persisted. Spur began walking. Vail was almost to the edge of the stamping mill. All the machinery was out in the open here. If the elements got too bad they simply stopped the stamping.

Spur fired a shot at Vail, who turned and looked at him, then ran on forward. Spur walked after him. No chance he could run again. The pain jolted him, but he gritted his teeth and kept moving.

The big wood-and-steel stamping units masked the small man a few minutes later. Spur couldn't tell if Vail was just behind the stampers or if he was running on for the mill. So he must have a partner in the mill or in the mill office.

Fairfax. Dooley Fairfax, the general manager of the mine. Who better to set up a swindle like this? He could hide the results of the test tunnels. He could cause one of the men to fall to his death. He could also be one of the vigilantes and order the lynching of Davis because he was a Southerner. The other hooded men wouldn't know the secondary reason for killing Davis.

It was worth checking out. Spur came closer to the stamping mills as the 30 heavy rod heads slammed into the ore at the bottom of their fall. The noise was enough to make him want to stuff cotton in his ears. A dozen men worked around the machines—some adding ore to the crushing boxes, some working the screens, some collecting the raw gold dust and small nuggets.

Spur saw one man near the far end look up with anger and fear on his face.

"Give it up, Vail," Spur called. At once he realized that no one more than two feet from him could hear what he said. He ran to the left around the machines. At once his rib throbbed with pain. He drove on, ignoring the hurt, angling to cut off the vigilante from getting to the mine office higher on the slope.

Vail took a few steps, saw he was bested, and turned back to the stamping mills, running between two of them and pulling out his gun. Spur was 30 feet away and figured that Vail wouldn't fire. Vail had only one round left and wouldn't use it until he had a sure shot.

Spur saw Vail talking to the men at the stamping mill. They looked at Spur and he ran straight for them. Vail dodged behind the group and sprinted to the side, where a few small pines grew.

Four husky miners blocked Spur's path between two of the tall stampers. He waved his Smith &

Wesson at them but none of them moved. He picked the smaller man on the end of the four, crashed into him with his right shoulder and bowled him over backward without losing his feet himself. Spur's chest daggered the new pain into his brain but he didn't waver. Two of the big men started toward Spur. He lifted his six-gun and fired a round in the air. They stopped, eyes wide, then backed up.

Spur charged ahead. Vail had skittered between two more of the big stamping mills and vanished. Spur started to go between the same two hammering structures, then darted back where he had been. Vail sprinted from between the next mill down, saw Spur, and screamed in anger. He yelled something but Spur couldn't hear him.

Spur lunged at the man, missed him, and sprawled on the square rack below the stamp mill, where the mashed-up ore came on to the screen. Spur threw out his arm to catch himself and his hand landed in the boxlike area at the bottom of the stamping mill. He jerked his hand out a fraction of a second before the heavy, two-inch-thick rod slammed down against the gold ore on the steel bottom of the mill.

A second more and his hand would have looked like ground meat. Spur stood and looked for Vail. The small man had vanished again. By now most of the workers had pulled back from the stamping mills and watched. Three of them stared at the next to last mill and talked among themselves.

Spur ran that way, fired once in the air, and saw Vail peer out from behind the big wooden beams. Vail pulled back and thrust his gun around the upright and fired blindly. The round missed Spur by ten feet. Spur surged to the stamping mill unit and ran around the heavy concrete base.

Spur didn't see the little man coming until nearly too late. Vail swung a two-by-four at his head. Spur ducked and lifted his six-gun. He wanted Vail alive. He shot him in the thigh. The heavy slug slammed Vail backward three feet and sent him sprawling over the shaking tray that separated the gold in front of the stamping mill.

Vail hit the screen hard and bounced backward. His head glanced off the side of the stamping mill and sideways into the stamping box of the mill on top of the rich gold ore. Before he could react, the heavy head of the stamping rod thundered down.

He had no time to scream. Blood, brain tissue, and bits and pieces of skull splattered over the box of gold ore. One of the workers screamed, ran to the body, and tugged it forward away from the stampers. Then he pulled the corpse down off the screens to the rocks and dirt in front of it.

Spur dropped to his knees. He'd never seen anything like that. There was nothing left of Vail's head to identify him, just a mass of pulp, blood, and skull fragments.

Spur looked at the battered body a minute, then shook his head. The stamping mills slowed and then stopped. The sudden quiet was deafening. The only real sound was the hiss and soft chugging of the steam engine at the end of the line of stamping mills.

Slowly Spur put away his Smith & Wesson, stood, and walked down the hill. The sun was out, the air mountain fresh and clear, the sky a brilliant blue. But none of it came through to Spur, who walked with a frown, slowly shaking his head. Vail was a vigilante who would have hung. It didn't matter how he died. It was an accident. It didn't matter at all how Odell Vail died.

Spur denied his own reasoning. He would never forget the sound when that steel rod stamped down and through Odell Vail's head. It did matter how a man died. It mattered a great deal.

Chapter Ten

It was a little before noon when Spur walked into the deputy sheriff's office and told him about Odell Vail. The deputy sheriff shook his head.

"Too much going on up here all of a sudden. I sent word on the stage yesterday for the sheriff himself to come up here and handle it all. It's over my head."

"You better go up and take a look at Vail and then call the undertaker," Spur said. "As for me I'm going to have a drink, maybe two or three."

Spur was on his way to the Deep Shaft Saloon when he saw a line of people in front of Odell Vail's office. He was curious. He went that way and talked to two men in the line.

"What's this all about? Somebody passing out free cash?"

The man in the line was grim faced. "Not at all. You must be new in town. The mine is closing next week. Everyone'll be out of work and the town is going down the creek. Odell is buying up land and property for twenty cents on the dollar. I figured I better get what I can now and have a little grub stake for our move to some other town where I can look for a new job."

"What do you do here?"

"I'm a clerk at the general store. Way I figure it I got about a week before Mr. Upton lays me off. He won't have no customers."

"How did you hear about this?"

"How? Everybody knows the mine is about bust. Then this morning Vail put up that sign in the window."

Spur turned and saw the sign. He hadn't noticed it when he had stormed in there before:

Moving? We offer you twenty percent of the value of your home or business in Gold Ledge. Cash money, right now. Bring your recorded deed, land grant, or homestead certificate. Offer good today only. Hurry. Tell your neighbors.

"Don't want to disappoint you men, but the mine isn't closing," McCoy said. "They found a new vein about a week ago. I don't know why it's been kept a secret. I saw it myself. The vein is hard white quartz a good three feet wide and loaded with gold. This town isn't closing down next week. That's for damn sure."

"How we know you ain't the one lying to us?" a man in the crowd asked.

"What do I have to gain?" Spur said.

"What did Vail have to gain?" another man asked.

"What if he knew the mine wasn't played out? What if he knew there was a fortune in gold still in it. If he could make you think the mine was played out, he could get your property for almost nothing. Then if you wanted to stay after the mine kept running, you'd have to buy your house back or pay him rent. Damn neat little swindle he was pulling here."

"The mine ain't closing down!" a man shouted. He ran down the street spreading the word.

Spur watched him. He should get Havelock to make it official, but that was out of the question. Maybe his daughter would do the job. Spur almost ran up the hill to the big house.

Nathan R. Havelock was no better. The doctor said he would try the smelling salts again about dark. Spur told Gwen what he wanted, and she agreed at once to go talk to the townspeople.

She dressed and they hurried down the slope to the middle of town. Spur fired his six-gun and bellowed, "Come and hear the good news. Mine is staying open."

He reloaded and fired six more rounds and repeated the message. He went into the saloon and brought out a poker table and chair, then helped Gwen to step from the chair to the table. By that time more than 100 people had crowded around them in the middle of the street.

Spur loaded and fired five more shots into the air; more and more people arrived. Gwen held up her hands for them to quiet down.

"Listen to me. I have heard a lot of rumors about the town closing because the mine was playing out. That's not true. We've just discovered a new vein that's three times as wide as the one we've worked here for almost four years.

"The town isn't closing down and neither is the mine. Don't sell your house or business to anyone. Hang on and, as soon as my father is better, he'll tell you himself. He was shot last night by some unknown gunman, but we're tracking the gunman down. Remember, the Gold Ledge Number One has a new life. It's going to be working gold for another five to ten years at least!"

A big cheer went up and the people broke up into small groups, chattering about the mine.

Spur went back to the boardwalk and found a new line in front of the real-estate office. There were about 20 men with angry faces.

"We been cheated by that no good Vail," one of the men bellowed.

Spur gathered them around and told them Vail was dead. "I don't think you have to worry about your property. I'll get the best lawyer in town to represent you. You sold your land and houses under a shroud of deceit and false notifications. Any judge in the land would back me up."

Spur scowled and folded his arms. "But that's going to take months. Why don't we work around that long wait? Let's go in and find the sale records and do some reversals. Each of you go and get every dollar that Vail paid you for your property and be back here in half an hour.

When they came back, Spur had found the record of the sales and the deeds, land-grant certificates, and homesteading papers. Odell Vail had been extremely businesslike, marking down the exact amount he had paid for each of the homes, stores, and lots he'd bought from the frantic sellers.

Spur knew what he was doing wasn't exactly following the letter of the law, but it was just.

Within a matter of two hours he had returned all the properties to the rightful owners for the amount of money they had been paid. In effect there had been no sale, no one got cheated, and the estate of Odell Vail was worth exactly what it had been worth that morning.

Spur closed Vail's office, locked the door, and began thinking about the other two vigilantes he hadn't yet identified. He still had his suspicions about the mine manager, Fairfax. He could also be a prime suspect in the shooting of Nathan R. Havelock. Spur headed up the hill to check on the mine owner. He hoped there had been some improvement.

Gwen must have seen him coming. She opened the front door for him and hugged him. Then she took him up to the second-floor master bedroom.

"Not much better. He sat up for a few minutes, looked around, and asked where he was. Then before I could even talk to him, he sighed and laid down. He hasn't made a sound since. I'm so frightened!"

Spur hugged Gwen tightly; then they went into the bedroom. Nathan R. Havelock lay on his bed, looking about the way Spur had seen him that morning. He breathed, twitched and turned, but he wouldn't wake up.

"Doc Gaylord stayed until about ten o'clock. He tried the smelling salts again. That didn't work. He and I talked loudly across the bed but that brought no more than a frown and a change in his position. Doc said to call him if Daddy wakes up. He said he might come to life anytime, or he might just—"

Spur turned her to face him. "I can't say that he'll be all right or that he'll be the same way he was before he got hurt. I think there's a chance. That's what we have to hope for now."

They heard the bed squeak and looked over. Nathan R. Havelock sat up in the bed and stared at them, a frown on his face.

"Damn but you two are whispering loud. How do you expect a man to get a good night's sleep with you chattering away like that? I'm so hungry I could puke. Gwen, get me some breakfast, will you? My usual: cakes, eggs, bacon, coffee, the works."

Gwen ran to him and knelt at his bedside. She put her arms around him and hugged him. "Daddy, I'm so glad you're feeling better."

"Feeling better? Why shouldn't I? Nothing wrong with me."

Spur frowned. "Mr. Havelock, do you remember me?"

The mine owner looked up. "Certainly, you think I'm addled? You're the young man who came to dinner. Something about some work on our little vigilante problem."

"Daddy, do you remember going to the mine office last night?"

"Office? Why would I do that?"

"Mr. Havelock, would you look at your chest?" Spur asked.

"My chest?" Havelock frowned and stared at Spur, then looked down at his chest. His nightshirt covered it. He started to lift the shirt and yowelled in pain.

"What the hell?"

"You were shot, Daddy. Do you remember?" Gwen said.

"Shot? Certainly not. I—but something does hurt." He lifted the nightshirt and stared at the bandage on his chest. "Be damned, somebody patched me up. Old Doc Gaylord?"

Gwen nodded. "Yes, you were shot by someone, but we don't know who. We want you to tell us who shot you."

Havelock shook his head. "Damn, am I losing my mind? I don't remember anything about being shot."

"It happens, Mr. Havelock. It's the shock of the wound sometimes, or maybe the shock of finding out someone you trusted was trying to swindle you. You don't remember who it was you went to the mine office last night to see?"

Havelock's face sagged and he blinked rapidly. He sniffled and shook his head. "I'm getting old and feebleminded. I'd say you're making it up, but I do have a lot of hurt now that I feel it better. Oh, damn."

Gwen went to the door. "I'll get that breakfast. Doc said you should eat anything and everything you want. I'll bring it up just as soon as Ling How can fix it. You talk with Spur."

Spur stood away from the window so Havelock could look at him without having to face the harsh light.

"Mr. Havelock, let me set up a situation for you. I want you to tell me what you'd do in such a case. Let's pretend that someone is trying to convince you that the mine is about played out, that it's worthless and due for scrapping. Who would you suspect of trying to swindle you that way?"

"Who? You mean the mine is not playing out? That someone is trying to convince me that it is, but it's still a profit-making gold mine?"

"Yes, I've seen the vein of ore. It's good white quartz and nearly three feet wide rich in free gold and veins all over the place."

"I came up figuring I'd have to shut it down. So it isn't true. You want to know who I think might try to swindle the mine from me. Only one man who would have the power and the chance to convince me it's played out. That would be my general mine manager Dooley Fairfax."

"Is he the man who shot you last night?"

"I don't know. I honestly couldn't tell you."

"Right after I told you about the new strike in one of the exploratory tunnels, you went storming out of the house with your derringer. I wanted to go with you, but you said you'd shoot me before you let me tag along. Then you stormed away and we found you in the mine office about an hour later. You were shot in the back incidentally."

"Oh, my God. And now I can't remember who tried to kill me."

"I think I'll have a talk with Fairfax." Spur told Havelock about Odell Vail trying to buy up town property for 20 cents on the dollar.

Havelock nodded. "I've heard about it happening before in mine towns. This would fit the pattern. Not only fake the closing of the mine, but cause a panic among the people in town so they would sell their property for a dime on the dollar. The man who swindled the mine from me would then own the mine and most of the property in town."

Spur grinned. "You sound like your old self again, Mr. Havelock."

"Except for my memory about last night when I was shot. My mind just refused to accept it and blocked it out somehow. Just hope to God I'm not going crazy."

"No chance of that. Where would Fairfax be about now? In the mine office?"

"More than likely. Or covering up some more fresh gold strikes in the mine. Damn, but I wish I could remember if it was him last night. You found me in the office. He would be the most logical one to be there. Him and the clerk, Jethro. Not a dishonest bone in that lad's whole skeleton. Couldn't have been him."

"I'm going to check on Fairfax."

It was late afternoon when Spur came out of the mansion and walked across the side of the mountain a quarter of a mile to the mill and the mill office slightly below it. He opened the door and went inside.

Only the clerk was there, the one Spur had seen before.

"Where's Fairfax?" Spur asked.

"Not sure, Mr. McCoy. He was here awhile early this morning when I arrived in fact. He was doing something in his private office. Then he asked me for the mail and I gave it all to him. He left just before noon, but I have no idea where he went."

"He hasn't been back since noon?"

"Not that I've seen and I've been here all the time."

Spur thanked him and went outside. If Halifax was running, he had a five-hour head start. Spur went back inside.

"Does Halifax own a horse?"

"Oh, no, sir. Said he didn't like to ride. Did only when he had to."

Spur thanked the clerk and headed across the slope to the mine manager's house. The front door was open; no one was inside. The dresser drawers had been emptied, some clothes scattered. A small desk had been left open with a few papers on it, but no books or records. The goose had flown.

Outside, Spur headed for the livery barn. Yale was dead but someone must be running the place. He found a short, thickset woman with a pipe in her mouth and spectacles on her nose. She stared at him and he figured she knew he was the one who killed her husband if she was Mrs. Yale.

"Yes, I rented a horse to Mr. Fairfax. He said he wanted to do a little riding just for fun. He didn't have no carpetbag or anything to tie on the saddle. Said he'd need the horse for a day or two."

"Thanks. You rent a lot of horses today?"

"Only the one. Business ain't so good."

"Which way did Fairfax ride?"

"He took the south trail down toward the creek. Ain't my job to spy on my customers."

Spur thanked her and picked up the prints of the big mount just past the livery door. He followed them on foot south to the creek, where they turned north and angled around town. Why would Fairfax want to do that?

Spur lost the tracks when they crossed Main Street between the stores and the last houses. After a brief search, he found the same prints on the other side of the street and stayed with them. They struck up hill, along a narrow little gully that could be a gushing torrent of water after a heavy rain.

The tracks crossed a rocky place and again it took Spur ten minutes to make sure the tracks went straight across. He looked up to be sure where he was and saw the Havelock mansion in the distance. It was higher on the mountain but not more than a quarter of a mile to the left. The tracks angled that way.

Was Fairfax back for vengeance? Why would Fairfax want to go to the mansion? He must know he had wounded and maybe killed Nathan R. Havelock. If Fairfax was the guilty party he must know that Havelock would probably tell who had shot him. Why would Fairfax go back?

Unless he wasn't the guilty party.

Then why would he have gone to the office before the usual time, left early, and cleaned out his house? No, Fairfax was leaving all right. Then why come back to the mansion?

Robbery or revenge. It had to be one of the two. Spur gave up his tracking. He had the end of the trail in sight and he ran forward at a steady trot that wouldn't hurt his broken rib, but let him cover ground quickly.

He was still 50 yards from the mansion when a rifle cracked in the stillness of the mountain air and a lead slug slapped into the dirt a dozen feet behind him. Spur dived to the ground and crawled to a three-foot-high boulder he could hide behind.

That one shot cleared up a lot of questions. Fairfax was the man who had shot Havelock in the back last night. He might have cleaned any cash and checks out of the mine office this morning, then started his getaway. But why had he come back to the mansion? Money or Gwen? He might have lusted after Gwen for years and never told her.

That was just speculation. How in hell could Spur get away from where he crouched behind the boulder and up to the mansion? He could risk zigzagging from cover to cover and hope to make it to safety. Or he could sit there for another half hour, let dusk fall, and run away from the spot with no danger.

Spur decided on both courses. Hard telling what Fairfax might do to the mine owner and his daughter in another half hour. Spur threw a rock to the right, then charged away from his protection to the left. He dived behind another big rock just as a lead slug ricocheted off his rocky protection and into the sky behind him.

He'd wait for dusk. He'd given Fairfax the idea that he was going to sprint for the woods, so the killer would have to be on the lookout all the time. He wouldn't be able to harass Mr. Havelock or get sexy with Gwen.

Dusk came slowly. When Spur figured it was dark enough, he charged away from his fort, changed directions three times, and crashed into the woods with no shots coming his way. He stormed upward to the last of the woods and then sprinted for the big woodshed built on the back of the mansion. He made it.

Spur panted as he rested against the shed. He shoved a sixth round into his Smith & Wesson and thumbed back the hammer. He heard nothing from inside. Back door, front door? The shot at him came when he'd been nearest the front door. He sidled around the building until he could see the back door and made a dash for it.

There was no reaction from inside. He bent low to the ground and opened the back door letting it swing wide. Nothing happened. He peered around the doorframe into an enclosed porch with another door straight ahead.

Gold Ledge Gold Diggers

He slipped across the wooden floor to the next door and was about to reach for it when a gun fired inside and splinters erupted from the thin doorway as a lead slug rammed through it.

Spur had moved up beside the wall next to the door. That one move had saved his life. He reached out and unlatched the door. Another bullet snarled through the thin wood. Spur pushed the door open and waited.

A moment later he looked around the frame from a foot off the ground. In front of him ten feet in the kitchen he saw Gwen sitting in a chair with Fairfax standing behind her with a gun muzzle at her head.

"Take one step inside and Gwen dies instantly," Fairfax said. "I know you can hear me. Throw out your six-gun and be quick about it."

Spur scowled. He had no shot. His upward angle left almost none of the man exposed. But he wouldn't throw out his gun. He spotted a half brick near his knees. He picked it up and threw it into the room so the gunman would have to turn to follow the sound.

As he threw the brick, Spur stood and looked around the doorway. The brick hit, bounced, and struck the wall. Fairfax turned and exposed his right shoulder. He moved the weapon to follow the sound. Spur fired. His shot hit Fairfax in the shoulder and drove him back.

Fairfax's left hand pulled the gun around, but the instant the brick sailed into the room, Gwen had jolted forward and dived to the floor.

Fairfax fired at the open door and made Spur duck back out of the way. In that moment, Fairfax darted through a doorway and out of sight. Gwen crawled over next to the wall with

141

the door Fairfax had just vanished through so she was out of any line of fire.

"Take her, McCoy. She's yours. I still have the ace to play that beats your hand. I have the old man upstairs with one slug through him. You keep chasing me and it'll be two or three more .44 rounds. Only these will be through his head."

Spur could hear footsteps in a room next door, then more running steps. He rushed to Gwen, lifted her, and hugged her.

"Did he hurt you?"

"No. He was threatening Daddy. I told Fairfax I'd go to bed with him if he just left Daddy alone. He didn't. He made Daddy get up and open the safe. He took the deed to the mine and ten thousand dollars Daddy always keeps in the safe. I don't know what he's going to do now."

"Stay here. I'm going to see if I can find him."

Spur slipped up to the doorway and looked through. He saw a small room with a large table, perhaps to arrange and assemble food on prior to serving it. He stepped soundlessly to the next door and found the dining room. He'd been there before. The open stairway was past another room toward the front of the house.

Nathan R. Havelock was on the second floor. Spur worked that way, made it to the stairway, and scowled at the open space with no cover.

Gwen came up behind him and touched his shoulder. He turned, and she motioned him to go with her. They ran lightly to the back of the house and she showed him a small, metal circular staircase that went to the second and third floors.

"A fire escape," she said. They hurried up the staircase and she opened a door that led to the second floor.

Gold Ledge Gold Diggers

As they peered out they saw Fairfax come into the hall and look down the open stairs. He had a six-gun in each hand now. The bedroom door he came from was where Nathan R. Havelock lay. The room was 30 feet from where Spur stood hidden behind the door leading to the circular stairs.

He motioned for Gwen to be still. Then he lifted his Smith & Wesson and steadied it on the doorframe with an inch of the barrel sticking out the door.

"We wait for him to come out again," Spur whispered. "He'll get nervous when he doesn't hear us. He can't afford to wait too long. Where does he have his loot?"

"It's all in saddlebags and in a small leather case he's tied onto the saddle."

"He should have kept going. It would have taken me two or three days to catch him."

They waited. Five minutes later, Fairfax came out of the room, looked both ways along the hall, then took three steps toward the stairs, both his guns ready. Spur steadied his sight, then squeezed the trigger.

The round hit Fairfax in his left shoulder and slammed him forward. Spur cocked the hammer and fired again, but Fairfax went down to one knee and fired twice at the door where Spur hid. McCoy had pushed Gwen down to the floor and then leaned against the solid wall before the shots came through the door.

Spur fired out the door again and saw Fairfax look back at the safety of the door he had left and then at the stairs. He chose the stairs.

Spur followed as closely as he could, getting to the top of the steps just as Fairfax made it

143

to the bottom. Spur tried another shot but the banister got in the way and deflected the round. Before Spur had another shot, Fairfax was out the front door and Spur heard hooves cutting into the ground.

Gwen ran up to Spur at the head of the stairs with a rifle.

"Got it from Daddy's room. It's a repeater with eight shots."

Spur raced down the steps and to the front door. He could barely see the horseman pounding downhill in the moonlight. Spur fired all eight rounds at the shape and the sounds.

A moment later he heard the shriek and scream of a horse in anguish. Then all was silent.

"The horse is down," Spur said. "I have a chance now to find him. Stay here with your father and lock all the doors and windows."

Spur raced into the night, reloading his six-gun and wondering just what the killer in front of him would do—run or hole up somewhere and fight?

Chapter Eleven

Spur raced into the darkness. He ran for 30 yards, stopped, and listened. He could hear someone groaning ahead. Was Farifax moving? Yes, footsteps, not running, not regular. The man might be staggering.

Spur ran toward the sounds again. Ahead the flash of a gunshot sparked in the darkness. A bullet whizzed by him a dozen feet away and wasted itself on the rocky slope.

Spur continued to move down the slope toward the gunman. He hoped that Fairfax had been hit by one of the rifle slugs or that he had been smashed up when the horse went down. Spur came to the silent form of the horse and went around it. He hated having to kill a horse, but it was much better to do that than let this murderer get away free.

Spur listened again. Fairfax had changed his

route and moved to the left. Spur looked that way and saw the lights of the house closest to the mine and farthest from Main Street.

Spur ran faster. If Fairfax got inside and took someone as a hostage it would be ten times as hard to capture him. Two minutes later, Spur heard a screen door slam, saw a shaft of yellow lamplight streak through an open door, then turn off as the panel swung shut.

Spur continued running to the house, slipped up on the nearest side, and looked in a window. The shades were not drawn. It was a bedroom, but no one was there. He went to the next window. A living room with one lamp burning, but no people. The next window opened on the kitchen.

He saw a fat woman standing at a stove. She had a wooden spoon in her hand. Behind her two young girls hovered close. One looked about 15, the other one 12. Both were crying. Somewhere just out of his sight, Spur could hear Fairfax bellowing at the women.

"Do as I say or you're all dead, you hear me? You, girl, lock and bar the back door. You, older girl, do the same to the front door. Move! Do it now."

The girls looked to their mother, who nodded. They both ran out of Spur's field of sight.

"Now, woman, do you have a shotgun in the house?"

The woman shook her head.

"Are you sure? If I find one I'll bend it across your head."

The woman took a deep breath and then nodded.

"Get the weapon and bring it here broken open,

you understand?" The fat woman nodded and waddled to a closet at the edge of the kitchen near the back door. She pulled out a Greener double barrel and broke it open. It was loaded. She took it to Fairfax.

The oldest girl came back and he glared at her. "You know where the Colorado Cafe is?" The girl nodded. "You get right down there and tell the owner that Fairfax is in trouble. He should come with you with a shotgun and a six-gun. You do that right away. If you fail to come back with the man, I'll slit your mother's throat. You understand me, girl?"

She nodded. "What's his name?"

"Kerwin Irving. He's got just one arm. Now get out the front door and have your sister bar it behind you."

Spur hesitated. Should he let the girl go? He had to; otherwise the woman would be hurt. All he needed was one good shot through the window. Up to that moment he hadn't seen Fairfax. He decided that it was by design. Fairfax was in a spot that could not be seen from either of the two kitchen windows.

When the younger girl came back from the front door, Fairfax said, "Woman, come over here. You any good on gunshot wounds. Easy now, I'll have this six-gun against your gut. One false move and you'll be worm bait by morning."

"I dug out a few slugs. Let me get my fish-gutting knife. It's the best," the woman said.

"You cut me too much, fat woman, and you're dead and your two daughters are naked and all mine. You understand."

The woman nodded. "I won't hurt you no more

than need be to get the slug out. You want some whiskey?"

"Take too long to do me any good. Just dig, and be damn careful. I want to use that leg again right soon."

Spur waited. He couldn't endanger the woman. As he leaned there against the house, he worked out a simple plan. It would take 20 minutes for the girl to get to the cafe and bring back the one-armed man. He must be the other vigilante. With any luck, the slug would be out of flesh within five minutes. Then Spur would make his move.

As Spur waited, a scream came from inside the house. Nobody showed in the kitchen except the youngest girl, who sat at the kitchen table, her head on her arms, her eyes wide and bright with fear and excitement.

"Goddamn it!" Fairfax bellowed. "You damn near cut me in half."

"Should have had the whiskey," the woman said softly. "That or pass out. Be easier on you. Slug is in there two inches. Gonna hurt like hell."

"Do it."

He screamed again; then a shot blasted inside the house. The woman backed into Spur's view, a bloody towel in her hands.

"Done. I got it. Let me get a sheet to tear up to wrap you up so you don't bleed to death. Right over here." She took a folded sheet out of a cupboard and walked out of sight toward Fairfax.

Spur slipped around to the other kitchen window and broke out one of the four-foot-square windowpanes with the butt of his Smith & Wesson. A shot jolted through the empty pane a moment later. Spur was already on his way to the front of the house, where he broke a foot-square glass in the front door. Then he ran back to the unbroken kitchen window and waited.

"He's out there," Fairfax shouted. "Stand in front of the kitchen window so he can see you. Tell him if he does anything else I kill you and your daughter first."

Spur watched the woman come in front of the window. She lifted the windowframe and shouted out what Fairfax had told her. Then she backed up and went out of sight to the left.

Spur thought of a dozen ways to get the killer out of the house, but every one had too big a danger element for the two women inside. Even smoking them out wouldn't work. Fairfax would shoot the women first, then make a break for it.

McCoy shrugged, went toward the front of the house, and walked 20 rods down the hill. He had to stop the other man from going inside. After that, he'd just play it by chance.

He heard the eldest girl returning before he saw her. He stepped in front of her and put his finger over his lips.

"I'm a friend," he said. "Where's Irving?"

"Who are you? Some wild man's holding my mother and sister."

"I know. I'm chasing him. I'll help you. Where's Irving?"

"He told me he wouldn't come. Said if Fairfax has himself in trouble it's his own doing. His trouble has nothing to do with the committee, whatever that is."

Spur grinned and held her arm as they walked toward the house's front door. "When we get to the front door, you knock and call out that you're both there. Your mother just took the slug out of his leg, so Fairfax won't be coming to the door. He'll send your younger sister. As soon as we get inside, you cover your sister's mouth with your hand so she won't give us away. You both stay in the front room. Understand?"

"Yes, but don't let him hurt Mama."

"I won't. Now knock and call out that you're both here."

She did. They heard footsteps, then the door came unbolted and swung open. The younger girl's eyes went wide when she saw them, but she didn't say a word.

"We're coming in now," the older girl called. Spur walked with heavy tread toward the kitchen door. Just before he got to the door he dropped to the floor and edged around the jamb so he could see into the kitchen.

Fairfax sat on a kitchen chair, one six-gun in his right hand. The fat woman stood to his right. His left leg showed a white bandage and blood-stains down his pants leg.

Spur fired at the gun, then lifted his sights and hit Fairfax in the shoulder with his second round. Spur clawed air to come to his feet and charge into the room. Fairfax had dropped the six-gun. He was on the floor reaching for it a foot in front of his right hand.

Spur drilled the hand with a .44 slug, nailing Fairfax's flesh to the floor and bringing a continuous scream of protest and pain from the mining engineer.

Sheriff Newman looked at Spur and then at the bleeding man he had in tow. "You're what kind of a lawman?"

"Federal. United States Secret Service. Put this man in your jail. I'm charging him with at least three counts of murder, plus kidnapping, child endangerment, assault on a federal officer, and half-a-dozen other felonies."

The sheriff was a little over 40. He wore town clothes, a big badge, and a pair of six-guns he probably had never fired. "Abner told me about you and what was going on up here. Looks like we may need two deputies up here after all. Oh, Abner, best you go round up the local sawbones and have him stop by and see us. Hate to get too much blood all over county property."

Spur waved at the sheriff. "Be back in a few minutes. One more man we need for the vigilante hanging express."

Spur had seen the one-armed man in the Colorado Cafe a dozen times. Kerwin Irving had seemed cheerful enough. Spur had heard that the man lost his arm in the Civil War, fighting for the North. It figured that he'd be one of the vigilantes.

The man was behind the small counter when Spur went in. He saw Spur and nodded, then slipped into the kitchen. Spur followed him. He found the vigilante taking one last drink from a bottle of whiskey at his small desk.

"Guess it's all over," he said. "Past time. Started out as a lark, run an Indian family out of town. Hell, no harm in that. Then it got a little more serious. I didn't want to hang that Southern man. Hell, I got no fight with them who was on the other side. Over and done with. Fairfax said it had to be done or half the whites in the South would be up here after our jobs. Still I knew it wasn't right."

151

He stood up. "I got no weapon. Ain't fired one at all since I got home form the war. Looks like I never will again."

Spur followed the man out the front of the cafe and said, "Can't say for sure, but if you testify against the others, the judge might go easy on you. Talk to the district attorney when you get into the county jail in Colorado Springs. Can't promise anything. But he might work out something for you."

A short time later, Spur knocked on the door of the Havelock Mansion and it opened at once. Gwen stood there, arms on hips.

"Well?"

"Got him," Spur said. "How is your father?"

"Better. Almost back to new, but not quite. Now he's complaining about the pain in his chest, so I know he's getting better. Doc Gaylord was up to see him a while ago. He said the bullet must have missed almost everything important. In two weeks Daddy should be up and tearing around again."

"Opening that new gold vein," Spur said.

"Finding a new mining engineer." Gwen looked at Spur. "Have you had any food since breakfast?" Spur frowned a moment trying to remember, then shook his head.

"Let's go to the kitchen and see what Ling How can fix for you. Oh, Daddy has back all of his memory now. It was Fairfax who shot him. Fairfax was looting the safe when Daddy found him there. Daddy turned around and said he'd forget it if Fairfax put the money back in the safe. That's when Fairfax shot Daddy in the back from six feet away."

The leftovers from the dinner table became a

feast and Spur ate until he couldn't face another fried chicken leg. He thanked Ling How, then went up with Gwen to see the mine owner.

Nathan R. Havelock was sitting up in his bed, talking with a tall, bewhiskered man in a black suit. Havelock waved at Spur and introduced him. "McCoy, this is Vance Ramsey, my lawyer here in town." Spur shook hands.

"Now, tell us, did you take care of Fairfax?" Havelock asked.

Spur told them about his fight with Fairfax. Both Havelock and Ramsey looked pleased when Spur added that Fairfax was in jail, waiting to be taken to Colorado Springs for his trail.

"We also wrapped up the vigilante committee," Spur said. "We have all five of them, two dead and the other three heading for Colorado Springs on murder charges, among other things."

Havelock nodded. "Damn good work, McCoy. Glad that little problem is behind us. Now, on to more important things. My lawyer here has drawn up an agreement. I want you to sign it right there on line three."

Spur frowned. "What kind of an agreement?"

"Never mind, just sign it. I already have." Havelock thrust a pen at Spur and gave him the two-page document. Spur held it up to the coal-oil lamp and started to read it.

He laughed softly and shook his head. "Mr. Havelock, I'm a federal law officer. I can't take gifts, presents, or gratuities of any kind. I certainly can't accept half ownership in Gold Ledge Number One."

"Hell, why not? If it hadn't been for you, I'd have sold it to that bastard Fairfax for ten dollars. You deserve a little cash for your work. Quit being a lawman. Sign the paper and you can go live in San Francisco or New York and circulate in the best society for the rest of your life."

Spur shook his head and grinned. "If that's what I wanted, I would be there now. My father is a wealthy New York businessman. I like it out here with the common folks. Glad your memory is all back. In a week or so you'll be chasing those Denver widows again."

"No, not for a while. Two weeks here, the doctor said. But I'll stay busy. Have to find a new man for the mine. Tomorrow night we're throwing a party for everyone in town. Lanterns and streamers, two halves of a barbecued steer, all the food we can eat and all the beer we can drink. Lots of singing and dancing and picking. We'll have a real jamboree on Main Street. Ramsey here is in charge of the arrangements."

"We'll get that going in the morning, Daddy," Gwen said. "Right now, it's time you get your rest. No arguments. Lie down and I'll turn out the lights."

Gwen and Spur escorted the lawyer to the front door and wished him a good night. Then Gwen hugged Spur seriously.

"I'm not letting you out of my sight again," Gwen said.

"What about your father?"

"The doctor gave him some sleeping powder. I mixed it an hour ago. He'll be dreaming of gold veins within ten minutes."

Spur kissed her lightly. "You are bad, Gwen. You know that. You're a naughty girl."

She kissed him back. "It took me a while to learn that naughty girls have the most fun. Now let me see that Daddy takes his sleeping powder.

Then you and I will go to the third floor and have a small party."

"But I should go tell Mrs. Davis that she's no longer in any danger. I don't want her to worry another night."

Gwen kissed him again, ran one hand up one of Spur's legs, and pressed against his crotch.

"Mrs. Davis knows what happened tonight already. Believe me, in a town this size you can't even belch without everyone knowing about it. You can pay her a social call tomorrow."

"You don't leave a man much choice."

"I certainly do." She picked up his hand and pressed it to her breasts. "You can pet me on the right or the left side. Take your pick."

He went up the stairs with her. She checked her father's room and found the glass with the powder in it empty and her father snoring softly. Gwen grinned as she came out of her father's room. She had her blouse half unbuttoned and finished the job as they walked down the hall to the stairs that led to the third floor.

Spur hadn't been up there before. Gwen took off her blouse and dropped it on the hall floor, then discarded her chemise as they went up the steps.

"Oh, I forgot to tell you, Spur McCoy. I've got a surprise for you that I think you're going to enjoy."

Chapter Twelve

Spur caught Gwen's hand and led her up the stairs, enjoying the bounce and jiggle of her bare breasts.

"You sure know how to dress," he said.

She laughed. "I like to dress for the part. Do you like surprises?"

"Any surprise you bring me, I'll like. Guaranteed. What is it?"

"You'll have to wait and see." Gwen reached over and rubbed the growing lump in his pants. "Yes, I think you'll enjoy it."

She led him down a short hall to a door on the third floor. He opened it and she went inside. Spur trailed along right behind her. It was a bedroom with an oversize four-poster bed and canopy. In the middle of the bed, facing away from them, sat a young woman with black hair streaming down her bare back.

Gold Ledge Gold Diggers

"Who is this?" Spur asked.

The girl turned slowly, showing that she was naked. Her small up-turned breasts came into view and crossed legs protected a swatch of black hair at her crotch. Her face remained turned away; then she slowly brought it around to look at Spur with a big smile.

"Ling How," Spur said. He looked at Gwen with a small frown. "I thought you said that you and I—"

"Oh, we will, darling Spur McCoy. All three of us will. Don't tell me that you've never had two girls at once?"

McCoy grinned. "A time or two."

The two women caught Spur and sat him on the bed, then began taking off his clothes slowly, enticing him all the way. Ling How reached across him and one of her breasts slid up to his mouth. Spur nibbled on the small nipple and watched it fill with hot blood and enlarge. Then he sucked her whole breast into his mouth and brought a gasp of pleasure from the small Chinese girl, who brought her other breast over for him.

By the time the women had him naked, Gwen had slipped out of her skirt and bloomers as well and all three of them bounced on the big, soft bed.

"Now this is a treat," Spur said. "But it does present a problem of how to make love to two lovely ladies at the same time."

Ling How looked at Gwen and both laughed. "We'll show you how," Ling How said.

Spur grinned. This was sex—no foreplay, no lovemaking, no soft tender words, no lies, no pretense, just fast, raw sex, the more the better.

Gwen lay on her back and spread her legs and

157

pulled Spur on top of her. She guided his erection into her glory hole, then she whispered to him and they turned over so she was on top. Slowly she began rotating her hips. Gwen's head lay on his chest and she kept working her hips to get him to a peak of intensity, then lifted and lowered, stroking him like a young heifer in heat.

At the same time Spur sensed something near him. He looked up and found Ling How on her knees beside his head. She smiled.

"You want to know how to make love to two women same time," she said. "Old Chinese custom: suck and fuck." She spread her knees and then reached over him with her hands and lowered her crotch over his face.

"I'll be damned," Spur said. "Somehow I never would have thought of this." Then she was there and he was drowned in the heat and musk from her pulsating outer lips. He brought one hand up, found the tiny node, and strummed it until she exploded in a writhing, humping, moaning climax that nearly smothered Spur. He pushed her up so he could breathe and she rolled away from him gasping and moaning and ripping into another climax.

Gwen lifted her head so she could see him. "What a sexy man. I hope you can do as good by me."

Spur began humping upward then, pounding Gwen's hips a foot off the bed into the air, driving again and again into her welcome slot, building her passion until she screamed in rapture and jolted into a climax that didn't end for nearly three minutes. She kept humping and shouting and spasming until Spur thought she'd break into a million fragments.

At last she tapered off and sighed and collapsed hard on top of him. She lay there a moment, then leaned up to look at him. "We forgot about you, darling Spur. It's your turn."

Spur rolled them over, lifted her legs high on his sides, and slid forward until he drove in all the way. He took a deep breath and pounded forward, slamming into her harder and harder. Finally, she screamed in another climax and he exploded a dozen times, smashing her into the bed and making the frame jiggle and rattle before he thrust the final time, let out a breath, and fell on top of her.

"My God, now that was a fuck," Gwen said.

Spur rested for five minutes, then roused, and sat up. He looked around for Ling How. She had been busy. A tray filled with a dozen kind of small cakes, desserts, and candies sat on a low table next to the bed.

"Nourishment," she said, "for a long night ahead."

"I'll eat to that," Spur said. The cakes and desserts were wonderful. He saved a special place for the chocolate candies. After he had eaten half of them on the tray, Ling How smiled.

"Aphrodisiac," Ling said and both women laughed.

"Hell, I don't need one. Not with two naked girls as pretty as you. What's next?"

"Stand up?" Ling asked.

"Been done. Not my favorite way."

"Ling How have new way. Old Chinese custom."

"I bet most everything is an old Chinese custom with you, Ling How. Let's see how we do this one."

159

She had Spur stand next to the wall, then went to his crotch with her hand and mouth and brought him to full erection quickly.

She leaned against the wall, put her hands around his neck and jumped up, locking her legs around his hips.

"So far nothing they don't do in Fargo, North Dakota, or St. Louis," Spur said.

Ling adjusted herself, held out his erection, and then gently impaled herself onto his shaft.

"Yeah, same stuff," Spur said.

Then she let go of his neck.

"Hey, wait a minute," Spur barked. "You're gonna break me in half."

Ling smiled and shook her head. She lowered her torso away from the wall and Spur didn't break in half but he felt a strange new sexual experience he had never known before. It was like 100 climaxes all at once. He shuddered and almost fell. Without using her hands or touching the wall, Ling How lifted her torso and the top half of her body to relieve some of the pressure on his erection.

Spur gasped in thanks but then she lowered herself again bringing another jolting spasm of incredible sexual release that Spur had never felt before. Twice more she came upward and then let herself down using only her stomach muscles to control her body. Each time the sensation was a new delight for Spur, thundering his being with a remarkable sense of delight and rapture. The last time Ling How came up all the way, put her hands around his neck, and gently disengaged from him.

Spur let her lead him to the bed and he slumped there. Then he fell over on his back, panting and shaking his head in surprise. It took him five minutes to recover. The girls sat near him chatting.

When he felt he could say something coherent, Spur grinned and shook his head. "How in hell did you do that? I've never seen anyone who had that much control over her body. Gwen would have smashed her head against the floor."

"Oh, yes, I would and brought you down with a busted cock. Ling How says it's all a matter of training and control and strength of stomach and torso muscles."

"If she did that one more time, I'd be a dead man right now."

"Ling How always knows how many times without killing you," she said, her black eyes sparkling, her long black hair half covering her small breasts.

"You get much practice doing that with the local boys?" Spur asked.

Ling How slapped him. She turned away angry and crying.

Gwen moved beside him. "Sorry, but Ling How is extremely sensitive about her sexual life. She is strict in her codes of conduct. She would never go outside of my house to do this. She works here and what we agree for her to do is fine, but she is not a dirty, ignorant Chinese girl who follows the railroad and fucks for money."

"Sorry, I just was so overwhelmed." He touched her shoulder. "Ling How, I'm sorry. You undid me. You splattered me all over the bedroom."

She turned back, her eyes troubled. "This is good?" She looked at Gwen, who nodded. Ling How's eyes brightened, her shy smile came back, and she turned to move closer to Gwen and Spur.

"Forgiven. Now what next?"

Spur laughed and moved to the tray. "I'm going to need some beer and some more of those goodies. You have any bottled beer in the place?"

"Yes," Ling How said. She jumped up and ran, her bare bottom swinging as she hurried out the door.

Gwen leaned back, letting her breasts flatten as she looked at Spur.

"Well, big spender. How do you like my little surprise for you so far?"

Spur reached for her breasts and caressed them tenderly, bringing a soft moan from her. "I like your surprise, and I think it's going to be a long, tough night between the sheets before I get both you ladies satiated."

The next morning, Spur had breakfast with the Haverlock family in their dining room. Nathan said he was well enough to get up, but Ling How took him a tray and insisted that he stay in bed the way the doctor ordered. He melted under her logic and ate as she watched him.

After the meal, Spur begged off, hurried down to the town, and knocked on Mrs. Davis's door. She opened it at once and smiled at him.

"I was hoping you would come by last night," she said. "I had a surprise for you."

"Well, thank you, Charlotte. I knew you'd hear that the last of the vigilantes was in jail or dead. You have nothing to worry about. I'm sure that Mr. Havelock will give you a generous death benefit, even though your husband wasn't killed in the mine. What will you do now?"

"Oh, you don't know. I met with Iona Ewing.

I'd known her before, but we got together to talk. Neither of us have kids, and we need to make some money, so we decided to open a boardinghouse. It was either that or start our own bawdy house, but we didn't really want to get into that line of work. Not that we couldn't if we put our minds to it."

"Sounds like a good idea. The mine will be good for another five years, at least."

"We're selling this house and using her place for the boardinghouse. We figure with some carpenter work, we can make seven bedrooms to rent. At five dollars a week, that would be thirty five dollars a week or a hundred and forty dollars a month. We should be able to set a good table for that and buy everything we need."

Charlotte closed the outside door and walked up to Spur. She touched his shoulders and edged closer until her face was an inch from his. He bent and kissed her and her arms went around him. The kiss lasted a long time; then she broke free and tears slipped down her cheeks.

"Oh, damn, I wish Lester was still alive. I miss a man so much." She leaned back. "I figure you're busy right now, but maybe later, before you leave town, you could stop by and see me one evening?"

"I'd like that. Just wanted to make sure you're all right." He kissed her nose and stepped back. "Now, good luck on your new venture, and I promise to see you before I leave town."

He checked in at the law office. Sheriff Newman was still there getting the paper work sorted out. He grabbed Spur, sat him down, and had him write out a detailed report on how the two vigilantes died. When Spur finished it, the sheriff read it over and had Spur explain two more things. After Spur had the document, the sheriff signed it as a witness.

The sheriff slouched in the one chair in the office and lit a cigar. "Looks like we have more than we need to convict the three on lynching charges. The one-armed man is turning state's evidence for a reduced charge. He won't hang at least. The widow Davis is going to testify as well. Looks like this about wraps up your part in the game."

"Almost. I still have some business up the hill with the mine owner."

Sheriff Newman grinned. "As well as his daughter. She's quite a handful with her dress store and all. Wouldn't be surprised if she opens a store in Colorado Springs."

The sheriff paused and held out his hand. "You did some damn fine work here, McCoy. I'll be sending a letter to your chief in Washington. Came for one job and ran into another one. Happens a lot in our line of work."

Newman paused again after shaking hands. "You going to be around town awhile? I could use a deposition or two on a few matters I'm not too clear on."

"I can stay a bit. Might call it a small vacation, but don't tell my boss that. Yes, I think a couple of days for some depositions would be good. You'll have the trial in Colorado Springs?"

"Probably. Would be better to have it here with all of the witnesses. But the jail just isn't big enough to hold the three men in one cell."

"Glad it's your problem, Sheriff. I'll see you tomorrow."

As Spur came out of the sheriff's office he

sensed a new spirit in the town. Four men were hanging banners across the street from one store to another. Fancy bunting and signs were going up on the one-block section that was most built up in the business district.

Two men stopped him and shook his hand.

"Hear tell that you saved the whole town," one said.

"Yeah, saved our jobs up at the mine and you saved me from selling my house for damn near nothing as well. Mighty glad to have you in town. Going to be a big shindig tonight. Food and music and dancing."

"Yeah," the first said. "We're on the committee to barbecue two halves of beef. Butchered a steer last night and it's hanging out now. Put it over the bed of coals about two o'clock for a feast around five."

"All the women are bringing scalloped potatoes, baked beans, salads, pies, and cakes. We're gonna have us a celebration that won't stop till tomorrow morning and maybe not even then."

"There's gonna be dancing too. We'll sweep part of Main Street free of dust down to the hard dirt and level it off for some good old country stampin'."

Spur told them to do a good job and worked his way through the unusually crowded street toward the far end. He had just passed one store when somebody yelled at him. He spun around, his hand near his six-gun. He saw Gwen with her head pushed out the door to her shop. She was motioning to him.

Spur went inside the shop and she marched him into the back and shut the door. She promptly pushed him up against the door and kissed him hard on his lips. Then she smiled.

"Hair of the dog, sexually speaking. Did we have a time last night or didn't we?"

"We did. I'm ruined for at least a month."

"Liar," Gwen said, rubbing his crotch. "I'd bet a tin mine that you could get it up right now if I was to encourage you with a few well-placed kisses."

"I need to talk a little business with your father. How's he feeling?"

"Better. He wanted to get up and go to the table for lunch, but I talked him out of it. He'll be roaring by tonight. He had six men in from the mine and talked to them. Picked one of the foremen to be the new temporary mine manager. Told the man, if he did well, he'd get the job permanently."

"Good for him. Always better in a business to promote from within. What about death benefits?"

"Most mines don't have them. Lots of deep-shaft mines lose one or two men a week in falls or explosions. I don't think more than three or four have died in Daddy's mine since it opened over three years ago."

"I'll go up and talk to him about it."

"The two widows?"

"Right. They're getting together to start a boardinghouse here in town. They figure there's a market now with the mine staying open."

Gwen walked up the hill with him to talk to her father. Nathan R. Havelock listened to Spur's proposal and nodded, waving one hand.

"Damn fine idea, McCoy. I'll set up bank accounts for the widows with a thousand dollars in each. Why didn't I think of it? Since you own half the mine, you're more than entitled to have a say in the operation."

"I don't own any of the mine," Spur said, frowning. "I didn't sign the contract, remember?"

"Oh, that. My lawyer drew up a new document you don't have to sign. Half of all the profits from the mine now go into an account with your name on it in the best bank in Colorado Springs."

"I don't want the money," Spur said.

"Too bad, it's in your name. I made an initial deposit of five thousand dollars to get it started."

Spur laughed. "You're a hard man, Havelock. Let me guess, I don't really own half the mine. I only own forty-nine percent of it, right?"

"I said I was thankful to you, not stupid. Actually you only have forty-five percent. But that should make you nearly half a million dollars a year from the new strike. Incidently, we set our whole crew to working that tunnel this morning. They're cutting the tunnel to seven feet high so we can get men and ore cars in and out easier. Should be showing a profit on the books on that vein within two or three days."

Spur shrugged and shook his head. "I guess I can't stop you from putting your money into any account you want. Oh, how about a schoolhouse? The town doesn't have a proper one. You can use part of my money to build a good schoolhouse. And then hire a schoolteacher who's been beyond the eighth grade herself. Be a nice bonus for your workers."

Gwen nodded. "Yes, Daddy, do that. I'll be so proud of you and the town will thank you."

Havelock grunted and stared at his daughter. "Can't turn my little girl down. Now get out of here and down to town so you can be sure the barbecued beef comes out well. I'll be down just before dark."

Spur grabbed Gwen's hand and they walked back down the hill.

"You going to be around town awhile, cowboy?" Gwen asked with a sly grin.

"Long enough to get into trouble. I'll do some depositions for the sheriff tomorrow and the next day. Then I'll go to Colorado Springs and wire my boss back in Washington. Gen. Halleck says he has a stack of jobs for me just waiting for my attention."

"Sounds fair. You promise me that you won't be out of my sight whenever you're not depositioning."

Spur grinned. "Promise. But you've got to make me a deal as well. Make sure that Ling How keeps her dress on. I nigh near came to dying dead away last night. This way I can concentrate on you."

Gwen grinned and grabbed his arm as they walked to Main Street. "Agreed, just so you don't dance with nobody but me when the fiddler plays and the banjo and guitar men get to do their picking."

Spur watched the town gearing up for a big party. It would be a wild night. He nodded his acceptance of the surrender terms to Gwen. But for a minute he was thinking about Colorado Springs and what the magic wire would bring for him to do next. There was almost always another job waiting. The West was a big place, and someday he'd have help in trying to bring it law and order. But for now, the Secret Service had just him west of the Mississippi to take care of business.

Spur felt that little itch on the bottom of his

feet. In one way he wished he were in Colorado Springs right now, standing outside the telegraph office and waiting for that key to start chattering.

He grabbed Gwen and they walked down to the twin pits dug into the middle of the street, where wood had been pitched into a fire to burn down to a huge bed of coals. Soon the beef would be suspended on iron bars across the fire and the sizzle of roasting meat would fill half the town. Already the town women were putting up tables. There would be enough food to feed an army.

Spur nodded. Yeah, this was the way a small town should be. He just hoped that the barbecue had enough of that thick sauce on it. Spur could almost taste it.

He and Gwen walked around town watching the activity. They helped string more streamers across the street and watched the beef cooking on the slowly turning spit. Each lent a hand turning the big crank to be sure the meat was cooked all through. They had five minutes; then someone else wanted to turn it.

Spur saw the stage pull in and stop short of its usual depot. In just a few days he'd be on board heading for a new problem. Oh, yeah! There wasn't any kind of work he'd rather be doing.

 **DIRK FLETCHER**

The pistol-hot Western series filled with more brawls and beauties than a frontier saloon on a Saturday night!

Spur #40: Texas Tramp. When a band of bloodthirsty Comanches kidnaps the sultry daughter of a state senator, the sheriff of Sweet Springs call on Spur McCoy to rescue the tempting Penny Wallington. Once McCoy chops the Indians' totem poles down to size, he will have Penny for his thoughts—and a whole lot of woman in his hands.
_3523-5 $3.99 US/$4.99 CAN

Spur #39: Minetown Mistress. While tracking down a missing colonel in Idaho Territory, Spur runs into a luscious blonde and a randy redhead who appoint themselves his personal greeters. He'll waste no time finding the lost man—because only then can he take a ride with the fillies who drive his private welcome wagon.
_3448-4 $3.99 US/$4.99 CAN

Spur #38: Free Press Filly. Sent to investigate the murder of a small-town newspaper editor, McCoy is surprised to discover his contact is Gypsy, the man's busty daughter, who believes in a free press and free love. Gun's blazing, lust raging, McCoy has to kill the killer so he can put the story—and Gypsy—to bed.
_3394-1 $3.99 US/$4.99 CAN

LEISURE BOOKS
ATTN: Order Department
276 5th Avenue, New York, NY 10001

Please add $1.50 for shipping and handling for the first book and $.35 for each book thereafter. PA., N.Y.S. and N.Y.C. residents, please add appropriate sales tax. No cash, stamps, or C.O.D.s All orders shipped within 6 weeks via postal service book rate. Canadian orders require $2.00 extra postage and must be paid in U.S. dollars through a U.S. banking facility.

Name _____
Address _____
City _____ State _____ Zip _____
I have enclosed $_____in payment for the checked book(s).
Payment <u>must</u> accompany all orders.☐ Please send a free catalog.

KANSAN DOUBLE EDITIONS
By Robert E. Mills

*A double shot of hard lovin' and straight shootin'
in the Old West for one low price!*

Showdown at Hells Canyon. Sworn to kill his father's murderer, young Davy Watson rides a vengeance trail that leads him from frontier ballrooms and brothels to the wild Idaho territory.

And in the same action-packed volume...

Across the High Sierra. Recovering from a brutal gun battle, the Kansan is tended to by three angels of mercy. But when the hot-blooded beauties are kidnapped, he has to ride to hell and back to save his own slice of heaven.

__3342-9 $4.50

Red Apache Sun. When his sidekick Soaring Hawk helps two blood brothers break out of an Arizona hoosegow, Davy Watson finds a gun in his back—and a noose around his neck!

And in the same rip-roarin' volume...

Judge Colt. In the lawless New Mexico Territory, the Kansan gets caught between a Mexican spitfire and an American doxy fighting on opposite sides of a range war.

__3373-9 $4.50

ROBERT E. MILLS

It takes a man with quick wits and an even quicker trigger finger to survive in a vicious world of fast guns and faster women—it takes a man like the Kansan. Get a double blast of beauties and bullets for only $4.99!

The Cheyenne's Woman. When Davy Watson's lovely lady is carried off by the vicious Cheyenne warrior Grey Thunder, the Kansan refuses to rest until he's rescued his beautiful lover. He heads for a showdown with the Indian that'll be a fight to the finish for one man—or both.

And in the same action-packed volume....

The Kansan's Lady. When his beloved Deanna is held captive by the ruthless Scotsman, Duncan Stearns, it's Davy Watson's last chance to even the score with Stearns and rescue his sweetheart. Either he saves Deanna—or he'll go down in one final blaze of glory.

_3450-6 $4.99

BUCKSKIN

By Kit Dalton

The hard-ridin', hard-lovin' Adult Western series that's got more action than a frontier cathouse on Saturday night!

Buckskin #35: Pistol Whipped. Rustlers are out to steal all the cattle in Oregon, and only Buckskin Lee Morgan can stop them. A six-shooter in one hand, a gorgeous gal in the other, he'll bushwhack and hog-tie the cow thieves—and mark all the lovely ladies with his burning brand.

_3439-5 $3.99 US/$4.99 CAN

Buckskin #36: Hogleg Hell. A demon-worshipping swindler is terrorizing Hangtown, California, and he has the lustiest lady in town under his spell. To save the tempting tart, Morgan will have to strike a deal with the devil's disciple—then blast him to hell.

_3476-X $3.99 US/$4.99 CAN

Buckskin #37: Colt .45 Revenge. Something is rotten in the state of Arizona, and Morgan has to put things right. Between hot lead and cool ladies, he'll have his hands full, his six-gun empty, and the Wild West exploding with action.

_3533-2 $3.99 US/$4.99 CAN

RED-HOT WESTERN ACTION
BY JACK SLADE!